PRAISE FOR AURORA ROSE REYNOLDS

"No other author can bring alpha perfection to each page as phenomenally as Aurora Rose Reynolds can. She's the queen of alphas!"

~Author CC Monroe

"Aurora Rose Reynolds makes you wish book boyfriends weren't just between the pages."

~Jenika Snow *USA Today* Bestselling Author

"Aurora Rose Reynolds writes stories that you lose yourself in. Every single one is literary gold."

~Jordan Marie *USA Today* Bestselling Author

"No one does the BOOM like Aurora Rose Reynolds"

~Author Brynne Asher

"With her yummy alphas and amazing heroines, Aurora Rose Reynolds never fails to bring the BOOM."

~Author Layla Frost

"Aurora Rose Reynolds alphas are what woman dream about."

~Author S. Van Horne

"When Aurora Rose Reynolds lowers the BOOM, there isn't a reader alive that can resist diving headfirst into the explosion she creates."

~Author Sarah O'Rourke

"Aurora Rose Reynolds was my introduction into Alpha men and I haven't looked back!"

~Author KL Donn

"Reynolds is a master at writing stories that suck you in and make you block out the world until you're done."

~Susan Stoker *NYT* Bestselling Author

When Aurora Rose Reynolds has a new story out, it's time for me to drop whatever I'm working on and dive into her world of outrageously alpha heroes and happily ever afters.

~Author Rochelle Paige

Aurora Rose leaves you yearning for more. Her characters stick with you long after you've finished the book.

~Author Elle Jefferson

Reynolds books are the perfect way to spend a weekend. Lost in her alpha males and endearing heorines.

~Author CP Smith

OTHER BOOKS BY AURORA ROSE REYNOLDS

The Until Series
Until November
Until Trevor
Until Lilly
Until Nico
Second Chance Holiday

Underground Kings Series
Assumption
Obligation Distraction

Until Her Series
Until July
Until June
Until Ashlyn
Until Harmony

Until Him Series
Until Jax
Until Sage
Until Cobi (Coming soon)

Shooting Stars Series
Fighting to Breathe
Wide-Open Spaces
One last Wish

Fluke my life series
Running into love
Stumbling into love
Tossed into love
Drawn in Love (coming soon)

Standalones
Falling Fast

Alpha Law CA ROSE
Justified Liability
Verdict
Finders Keepers

UNTIL HIM *BOOK THREE*

Aurora Rose Reynolds

M A Y

James Trevor

Trevor & Liz

Asher & November

Hanna
Cobi

July
June
May
December
April

James
Dean
Tia
Conner

B E L I E V E   I N

S   O   N

Susan Elizabeth

Cash & Lilly

Nico & Sophie

Jax
Ashlyn

Hope
Jasper
Edward
Toby
Destiny

Willow
Harmony
Bax
Talon
Sage
Nalia

Ava
Lillian
Alistair
Nash

THE   BOOM!

UNTIL HIM *BOOK THREE*

Hadley — Cobi

Cobi

Prologue

"Do you know her, Mayson?" my partner Frank asks, studying me and the woman in my arms. His shaggy brows are drawn tightly together in confusion over his blue eyes.

I want to roar, *"Yeah, I fucking know her. She's* mine*!"* but that would sound ridiculous, because it is fucking ridiculous. I don't know anything about the woman I'm holding besides the fact that her first name is Hadley, she smells like peaches, and she feels perfect against me, even if she is passed out.

"She yours?"

"No," I growl, my teeth grinding together as my hold on her tightens.

Getting closer, Frank drops his voice. "Then maybe you wanna stop fucking growling anytime one of them—" He jerks his thumb over his shoulder. "—tries to touch her, and let them do their job."

I frown and look past him, noticing the three paramedics standing around me looking unsure and nervous. I don't want to—*as in really fucking don't want to*—let Hadley go, but I know I need to. She has a cut on her forehead that hasn't stopped bleeding, and bruising under her jaw. I jerk up my chin, and one of the paramedics comes forward. I must make a noise, because his head flies my way when he touches her and his eyes widen with fear when they meet mine.

Fuck.

My jaw clenches as I force myself to relax and release her, and I watch with my breath locked in my chest as she's placed on a stretcher. It takes every ounce of self-control I possess to not go after her, to not reach out and touch her again just to prove she's real. As they load her in the back of the ambulance, I wrap my hand around the back of my neck. I want to go with them to make sure she's okay, but I can't. I have a crime scene that needs to be locked down and a dead body in the woods behind me that needs to be dealt with. The good thing is, since I'm a cop, I won't have a problem tracking Hadley down, even if she's released from the hospital tonight before I can get to her.

"What the fuck was that about?" Frank questions from my side as the ambulance doors shut and the lights go on.

I don't look at him. I run my fingers through my hair and shake my head. "Nothing."

"You sure you don't know her?"

"I don't know her," I mumble then look around. "Let's get this shit sorted."

"Fuck." Frank looks around the mostly dark woods and at the other officers milling about. "It's going to be a long night. I need to call the wife to let her know I won't be home for a while."

"When you're done with that, meet me at the body," I say, and he jerks up his chin before walking off. I grab a flashlight from one of the cruisers then head into the woods to get to work. When I got the call from dispatch informing me that a woman called 911 saying she witnessed an unconscious woman being dumped into the trunk of a car outside the local movie theater, I had no idea the unconscious woman was my cousin Harmony. Not until her sister Willow called to say Harmony hadn't returned from the restroom, where she had gone during the movie they were watching.

After Willow's call, I had dispatch connect me to Hadley, who was the one who witnessed my cousin's kidnapping. She was following the car, and I was close behind her—just not close enough. After she informed me that the car turned off the road, I told her that she should keep driving, that the other officers and I were closing in and would be there, but she didn't listen. Instead, she hung up and kept following. From what I learned, she ended up running for her life along with Harmony, who had somehow managed to escape the trunk of the car she was in. They both barely escaped death at the hands of a madman who was aiming a gun at them in the middle of the woods.

When I make it to the body, which is now covered in a white sheet, I know Frank was right. It's going to be a long fucking night. Only, unlike him, I have no one to call to tell I won't be home.

Four and a half hours later, the crime scene guys leave along with the coroner, and I catch a ride back to the station with Frank, where I pick up my truck before heading to the hospital. When I arrive, I check in at the nurses' station and ask about Hadley. I find out she suffered a concussion and that the doctors are keeping her overnight just to be on the safe side.

After being told she's resting, I go check on my cousin Harmony, who is out of surgery with our family gathered around her. I talk to my family and Harmony's fiancé Harlen for a few minutes, making sure they're good before I go to Hadley's room. It's across the hospital, and when I reach her door, I walk straight in, expecting to see her family gathered around her, but the room is empty except for the bed, where I can make out her form under the covers.

I take a seat in the chair next to the bed and stare at her face—like the stalker I've suddenly become. Even with dark circles under her closed eyelids, a bruise, and stitches marring her forehead, her features are elegant. She's beautiful, with dark, wavy, red hair that is fanned out around her head, and a peaches-and-cream complexion that is a stark difference to the white pillow she's lying on and the blanket she has pulled up under her chin.

I frown, wondering who she is and why she seems to have such a profound effect on me. I rub my hands down my face and lean back in the chair, too tired to think about that right now. I've been up since 5:30 a.m., and it's already after three the next morning. I tell myself I'll just rest my eyes for a minute then I'll leave and go home, but instead, I end up passing out.

3

"I cannot believe I had to find out from the news that you were in the hospital!" a woman shouts, jolting me from sleep. I sit forward, rubbing the back of my sore neck, and watch a very pretty woman with dark skin and long, wavy hair stomp across the room in heels toward Hadley's bed, where she stops to plant her hands on her hips.

"Brie, keep your voice down."

"Don't tell me to keep my voice down, Hadley. You're all over the news and in the fricking hospital."

"Yes, but as you can see, I'm fine."

"You were shot at!" the woman shrieks, and I wince at the sound then watch both women turn to look at me. "Who is he?" she asks Hadley then looks back at me, repeating her question with narrowed eyes. "Who are you?"

"Detective Cobi Mayson," I respond, and her eyes widen while her mouth forms a soft *O*.

"Do I need to make a statement?" Hadley asks before her friend can say anything, and I focus my attention on her, really seeing her for the first time in the light of day. Her small white teeth are nibbling nervously on her plump, pink bottom lip. Her wavy, shoulder-length hair is not dark red like I thought last night, but deep brown with a hint of red. She has a smattering of freckles across the bridge of her nose, and her eyes are blue, not a deep blue but a misty sea blue with flecks of gold that shoot out from the irises. "Do I?"

I clear my throat and play back her previous question in my mind. "Yes," I answer, figuring it would seem strange for her to wake up with me in her room for any other reason.

"He's dead, right?" she prompts, and I watch every muscle in her small frame tighten. "The guy who kidnapped that woman, Harmony— he's dead, isn't he?"

"He's dead," I confirm softly.

Her shoulders relax, and she whispers, "Good." Even though she says it like she means it, I can tell that her being relieved someone is dead doesn't sit well with her. Harlen told me that both Harmony and Hadley witnessed him killing Hofstadter with a bullet to the back of the head while he was standing over the two with his gun aimed at them

4

and his finger on the trigger. I have no doubt that if Harlen hadn't taken Hofstadter out when he did, neither my cousin nor Hadley would be here right now.

Looking into Hadley's eyes, I can see that what she witnessed last night is still messing with her. Most civilians will never be the victim of a violent crime, but those who are carry that weight around with them every fucking day, never able to put what they experienced behind them without a lot of time and some major help.

"Is… is… Harmony okay?" Her fingers wrap around the edge of the blanket so tightly that her knuckles go white.

"Harmony's good, out of surgery and resting. The doctors expect her to make a full recovery."

"Thank goodness," she whispers, releasing the blanket as her friend reaches over to rub her shoulder.

"Thank God you're okay too," Brie says, and Hadley looks up at her.

"I know," she agrees, and an uncomfortable feeling fills the pit of my stomach, one that has everything to do with the fact that I could have lost her before I even knew who she was to me.

"You shouldn't have followed them," I say. Her head turns toward me and her back instantly goes ramrod straight.

"Damn straight she shouldn't have followed them," Brie adds, but Hadley's eyes stay locked on mine.

I think I like Brie.

"I had to."

"I told you I was right behind you. I told you to keep fucking driving," I growl, unable to keep control of the rush of emotions filling my stomach and chest.

"And I told you I couldn't do that."

"You should have listened to me."

"Are you going to arrest me for not listening?" she asks, and I'm actually taken aback by the amount of attitude she's giving me. Most people don't talk back to me, and women never give me attitude unless I'm telling them that things between us are ending and it's time for them to move on.

"No, but maybe I should spank you for not following an order and for

5

putting yourself in danger," I reply.

Fuck. Why did I say that?

She inhales a sharp breath while Brie does the same. "I can't believe you just said that," Hadley hisses, pointing at me.

"Believe it," I return, watching her eyes that are still locked on mine change from misty blue to deep green while her cheeks turn pink with aggravation.

Fuck, she's beautiful when she's pissed.

"Well, this is interesting," her friend says, breaking our stare down, and we both turn our heads in her direction at the same time.

"Don't you need to leave for work?" Hadley snaps at her.

"I'm not going to work today. I'm staying here with you."

"No, you're not," Hadley denies with sharp jerks of her head.

"Yes, I am."

"No, you're not. I'm going to be lying in bed all day. You don't need to be sitting here staring at me."

"I won't stare at you. I'll read a magazine." Brie shrugs casually.

"Brie, you have to go to work. You know and I know that you can't miss any more days," Hadley says, and Brie's eyes narrow.

"It'll be okay if I miss today."

"You know it won't," Hadley insists. "Marian is looking for a reason to fire you. You miss today, you give her that reason."

"She can shove it."

"Brie." Even not knowing Hadley, I can hear the warning in her voice. "Go to work. You have a job to keep and a wedding to pay for."

"Fine," Brie grumbles. "I'll go to work, but only because I know you need rest and won't do that if I'm here." She leans over, wrapping her arms around Hadley and saying quietly, "I'm seriously glad you're okay, but I'm also really mad at you."

"You'll get over it."

Brie shakes her head, standing and pulling her purse higher up on her shoulder. "Let me know if they release you today. If they do, call me and I'll be back to pick you up."

"Don't worry about me. I'll be okay. I can catch a cab home if they let me go," Hadley says.

"You better call if they release you," Brie repeats more firmly, planting her hands on her hips once more. "I'm serious, Hadley."

"Fine, I'll call," she agrees, sounding reluctant.

"Rest," Brie orders, and then her eyes come to me. "Detective, don't give her too hard of a time." Then she's gone, and Hadley and I look at each other once more.

"Your friend's a little crazy."

"She's been my best friend since we were ten. She's like a sister to me."

"She loves you."

"We make each other crazy, but love each other unconditionally. She worries about me all the time," she says, starting to lie back down, and I see her eyes fill with pain.

"You want me to call the nurse to get you some meds?" I question softly.

"Do you have multiple personality disorder?"

I grin at her smart-mouth comment. "I don't think so."

"So you don't know if you do or not."

"I've never had a doctor tell me it's something I need to have checked out."

She sighs, lying back fully and wincing.

"Let me call a nurse in here. They can give you something to help with the pain."

"I'll be okay." She turns her head to look at me. "Where's your notebook?"

"Pardon?"

"Your detective notebook… to take my statement. Where is it?"

"I don't have one," I lie.

"Hmm." She looks at the ceiling once more, then asks quietly, "What do you need me to tell you?"

"Nothing." I stand and look down at her. "Not right now. Your friend was right—you need to rest. I'll get your statement later." Her eyes study me while her teeth nibble on her bottom lip again. "We'll talk soon, Hadley." I pull out my wallet from my back pocket and flip it open, taking out one of my cards. "That has my cell number on it. Use it. Call if you need anything, even if it's just to talk." I hand it to her.

"Thanks." She takes it, clutching the card against her stomach.

"What you did was stupid." Her eyes narrow on mine then widen as I skim my fingers down her soft cheek. "Stupid, but really fucking brave. Rest. I'll see you soon." I turn and leave without a backward glance, wondering just how long I will be able to stay away.

My guess? Not fucking long.

Chapter 1

I STARE AT THE TV in the corner of my room and pull in a shaky breath when another image of the outside of the hospital I'm in appears on the screen. My eyes close briefly when my name along with Harmony's is mentioned once again by the news broadcaster. Until I turned on the TV in my hospital room after Cobi left, I just thought I witnessed a crazy man kidnap a woman and that I did what anyone else would have done—attempt to help someone in need. I had no idea what happened to Harmony and me would make national news. I didn't know that the man who kidnapped her was a doctor at this hospital, a hospital she worked at as a nurse.

Dr. Hofstadter, the man I saw die last night, was involved in a dozen or more sexual harassment complaints that had been swept under the rug for years. Instead of Hofstadter being reprimanded like he should have been, his family—who were on the board of directors—fired almost every nurse who made a complaint against him, to hide what was going on. This went on for years until he made advances toward Harmony, who set out to bring to light what was happening. That's why he kidnapped her. From what the news said, he thought if she disappeared, so would the truth about what he was doing. No such luck.

Even from my bed, I can see what looks like ten news vans parked along the street with the satellites on top pointing at the sky. News anchors and cameramen are set up on the grass and sidewalks, stopping almost every person who walks out of the hospital. I have no idea how I'm going to get out of here without being questioned by the media, and I really do not want to be asked about a situation I know nothing about. For me, what happened to Harmony and me last night is a completely different story than the one that happened to her here at this hospital, but I don't think the media cares about the semantics.

"Both women were shot at as they ran for their lives," the anchorwoman says, and I quickly press mute as a shiver slides down my spine and fear fills the pit of my stomach. I do not need the reminder of what happened, of what *could* have happened.

"Knock, knock. Can we come in?" I look across the room at a man and woman I don't know standing just outside my open door. The woman is pretty, with long dark hair, wearing a simple white tank, a long beige cardigan thrown over it, dark jeans, and boots that go up to her knees. I notice she's holding a large bouquet of flowers and six or more Get Well Soon balloons tied to the vase with different colored ribbons. The man with her is scary hot, with a faux-hawk and tattoos covering almost every inch of his exposed skin. He's also huge, his tight white shirt and jeans showing off that, even for an older gentleman, he takes care of his body.

"I think you have the wrong room," I say, when the woman smiles and starts to come closer to my bed where I'm sitting.

"Are you Hadley?"

"Yes."

"I'm Harmony's mom Sophie. This guy is Nico, her dad."

"Oh." I look between the two of them once more. "Nice to meet you both."

"You too." Sophie sets down the flowers she's holding on my bedside table. When her eyes come back to me, she starts to speak. "I just…. We just want to say thank you for what you did last night."

Before I can reply, she grabs my upper arms and pulls me in for a hug.

12

"You're welcome." My words are muffled against her top, and I think I hear Nico chuckle.

"How are you feeling?" She leans back to look me over, and my throat starts to feel funny.

"I'm okay."

"Are you sure? Cobi mentioned you were in a little pain."

"Cobi?" Why is she mentioning Cobi? When I woke up and saw him asleep in the chair next to my bed, I thought I was imagining things. I didn't know Cobi in school, but like every other girl, I knew *of* him. I was a freshman when he was a senior, and he was always the topic of conversation, since he was not only gorgeous, but also nice to everyone, got really good grades, and played football. He was the quarterback of the team three years in a row, and everyone thought he'd play ball in college then go pro one day, because he was that good. Instead of doing what everyone thought he'd do, he joined the military right after high school, and even after he was long gone, people still whispered about him. Some said he was a hotshot sharpshooter. Others said he was in the Special Forces. I don't know if either of those things were true; what I do know is when I'm in the same room as him, my stomach feels like it's going to come up the back of my throat and my mind stops working properly, making me act like a complete idiot.

"Harmony and Cobi are cousins," Sophie says, not knowing my thoughts. "Cobi stopped by to check on Harmony on his way out. He told us you were still here, that you were in some pain, and to make sure you were looked after."

"Oh." I look between them. "The nurse gave me some Tylenol not long ago. I'm already feeling better."

"Good," Sophie replies softly.

"How is Harmony? I've asked about her a few times, but no one has given me any information."

"She's awake; she's okay. She's been worried about you."

"Please tell her I'm okay and that I'm glad she is too."

"I will," she agrees softly.

I look from her to Nico when he mutters a quiet "Fuck," then follow his gaze across the room to the television and my crappy old Facebook picture that's on the screen. "Someone leaked both your names to the media," he says, looking down at me. "The hospital has promised to find out who did it and deal with them, but as you can see, they're already running with the story." He could say that again. "Are you being released today?"

"As far as I know." I shrug one shoulder ever so slightly. "My doctor came in earlier and said I should be okay to go home, but he hasn't been back again."

"Do you have a ride?" I think about Brie and the look on her face earlier. If I don't call her to pick me up, she will lose her mind and I will never hear the end of it.

"I have a friend who will come pick me up once I'm released."

"Right," he mumbles and pulls out his phone. I watch him type something, and then less than ten seconds later, his phone beeps and he looks at me once more. "All set. Once your doctor says you can go, an officer will be here to escort you out to the staff parking lot. You can have your friend pick you up there."

"Thank you." My muscles relax—actually, my whole body relaxes at the news that I won't have to go out front and face the cameras.

"Anytime, and I'm sure Cobi will take care of you. But if you need anything, I'll give you my number. Don't be afraid to call."

"Thanks," I murmur, ignoring the Cobi taking care of me part, since after today I will hopefully never see him again.

Nico smiles a strange smile, like he knows something I don't.

"We're going to go and let you rest," Sophie says, grabbing my hand and attention. "But when Harmony is up to it, I'd love to have you join us for dinner."

I study her and her husband then think about what happened last night with Harmony. It's not a lie when I say, "I'd like that."

"Good." She leans over to kiss my cheek then, surprising me, Nico does the same. My throat itches as I watch them leave my room talking quietly and holding hands. I wonder if Harmony knows how lucky she is to have two people who obviously love each other and her; I hope she does. As a child of parents who can barely stand each other and couldn't care less about me, I know that kind of love is rare.

"You're free to leave, but I want you back here in a couple days so I can look at your stitches," Dr. Ross says, jotting something down in my file before meeting my gaze. "But if you have any nausea or if your headache gets worse, you need to come back to the emergency room."

"Sure," I agree, then I look toward the door when someone comes into the room. I take in the older gentleman and let out a relieved breath when I see a badge clipped to his belt. I also see he's carrying my purse and a white plastic shopping bag in one hand.

"Don't forget to come back. Normally there is nothing to worry about after getting stitches, but from time to time, infection can set in, and I want to make sure that doesn't happen," Dr. Ross adds, pulling my attention back to him.

"I'll be sure to come back," I assure him, as the officer comes closer to my bed and Dr. Ross looks at him.

"Detective Frank, this is Ms. Emmerson. They told me you'd be in to escort her out of the hospital. I appreciate it. Things have been a mess since the story broke."

"Anytime," Detective Frank replies, giving me a small smile before he looks at Dr. Ross. "It's going to be a while before the story dies down. You might wanna get a couple more security guards on the front door to manage who's coming into the building. I stopped one reporter on my way up and sent them back outside."

"I'll talk to the head of the security department and see what they can do," Dr. Ross says, looking annoyed. I can't say I blame him; I'd be annoyed too if my place of work was overrun with media.

"Let me know if you need my captain to make a call."

"Will do," Dr. Ross tells him, and then his eyes come back to me. "Take some Tylenol when you get home, and rest. I'll see you in a couple days."

"Sure."

He lifts his chin toward me then does the same to the detective before he leaves.

"Mayson wanted to come himself, but he's tied up on a case," Detective Frank says, and I focus on him, blinking in surprise. Why would Cobi want to come himself? "He also gave me this to give to you." He hands me my purse and the plastic shopping bag.

I open the plastic bag, seeing a pair of sweats and a plain white shirt. Cobi sent clothes for me? What the heck?

"He didn't have to do this." I hold up the T-shirt. "My friend would've brought me clothes when she came to pick me up," I inform him.

"We spoke before I came here. We think it'd be better if your friend doesn't come inside to pick you up, and Mayson doesn't want you having to wander the hospital in that gown or to have to go home in it." Okay, there was a lot there to take in, but before I have a chance to reply, he continues. "He also said you still need to give your statement. You up for that right now?"

I'm not really up for it, but still I want this done. "I'd like to get it over with."

His face softens. "How about you call whoever is picking you up then go change. We should be done by the time they get here."

"Right." I dig into my purse and pray my phone is there, and then pray it's still charged. When I see it is, I call Brie to let her know I'm being released, and Frank tells me where she should meet me. When I hang up with her, I go to the bathroom, taking the plastic bag with me.

I change quickly, ignoring the fact that the shirt smells like what I imagine Cobi would smell like—mysterious and masculine. I also ignore the fact that both the shirt and sweats are huge on me, meaning they possibly belong to him. It's odd enough that he sent something for me to wear; I don't think I could handle knowing they actually belong to him. After I'm dressed, I sit with Frank, who records my statement while writing it down in a spiral notebook that he pulls from his back pocket. When we're done, just like what was promised, I'm escorted through the hospital and out a back door to where Brie is waiting for me.

"Have your parents called?"

At Brie's question, I finish buckling my seat belt then look at her. "No." And they haven't. I got a couple of messages from people both Brie and I work with, but nothing from my parents. It's not surprising.

My mom and dad either don't know what's going on, or are so high and drunk they don't care about what happened.

"Seriously?" she asks, putting her car in reverse and backing out of her parking spot right next to the door I just exited through.

"They never call me unless they need something," I remind her, and her face tightens in anger.

"Your face is all over the news, along with the fact that you were shot at. Ken has been calling me all day asking if I've heard from you. He's worried, and you know he never worries about anything." She's wrong; Kenyon, her fiancé, worries all the time. Maybe not about day-to-day crap, but he's protective of the people he cares about, and because I've been best friends with Brie since forever and have known him since they started dating when we were freshmen in college, he's protective of me too.

"Kenyon also cares about me. My parents don't and they never have."

"You're their daughter, their daughter who could have died last night." She hits the steering wheel in frustration.

"My parents aren't like your mom and dad were, Brie. You know that."

"Have I told you how much I hate them?"

"Not long ago, you went off on an hour-long rant about how much you hate them. So yeah, you've told me," I mumble, and she glances at me and frowns.

"I do not rant. What is with you and Ken saying I rant all the time?"

I don't reply, because I seriously am not in the mood for her to start ranting right now. "Um, where are we going?" I ask when we miss the turn for my street.

"I'm taking you home with me. Ken and I want you to stay with us until we know you're good to be on your own."

"I'm not staying at your place."

"Yes, you are."

"Brie, I love you to death. You are the sister I never had. But there is no way in hell I'm staying with you and Kenyon. You only have one bedroom, and a couch that was made to look at, not made to lounge on."

"Our couch is comfortable," she argues, knowing that's an out-and-out lie. It's a beautiful, white leather couch, but it's hard as a rock and seriously uncomfortable to even sit on.

"No, babe, it's not. Remember a few months ago, when we got drunk and I passed out at your place? I ended up sleeping on the floor, because it was better than your couch."

"You told Ken you must have drunkenly rolled off the couch when he found you on the floor the next morning."

"I lied. I didn't want to tell him that your couch sucks."

"So you're telling me my couch sucks now?"

"Well, yeah, since I really do not want to sleep on your couch or on your floor. I want to sleep in my own bed tonight." *Or at least lie in my own bed tonight,* I think but don't say.

"Ken is not going to like this," she mutters, turning on a road I know will lead to my place.

"He'll be fine."

"He going to want to see you, want to see for himself that you're okay."

"You guys can come over when he gets off work. I just want to be home tonight."

"Fine." She turns onto my street then pulls in and parks in my driveway.

"Don't be mad," I say as she shuts off the car and unhooks her belt.

"I'm not mad," she huffs, opening her door. "I'm worried about you." She gets out, grabbing my bouquet of flowers before slamming her door. I do the same, but instead of slamming the door, I let out a sigh as I shut mine then follow her to the front door, where I use my key to let us both inside. I listen to her continue to rant, hoping it won't last forever as I drop my purse and kick off my shoes. "You didn't even tell me you were in the hospital. I had to see that on the news this morning when I was getting ready for work."

"I'm sorry. I was out of it, but you're right. I should have called as soon as I was able to reach the phone."

"You should have," she agrees, going to the kitchen, where she deposits the flowers before opening the fridge, grabbing a bottle of water, and handing it to me. "Drink that." I don't argue with her. I open the bottle and take a drink. "I really don't like that you want to stay here alone."

"Brie, the guy who chased me through the woods with a gun last night is dead. Very dead. He's not a threat." Bile slides up the back of my throat as an image of Hofstadter with a hole in his head and the life blinking out of his eyes fills my mind. "I'm safe."

"I know, which is the only reason I'm being cool about you staying here alone," she murmurs, studying me with tears filling her eyes.

"Please don't cry."

"I'm not going to cry," she lies, and I roll my eyes then go to her, wrapping my arms around her waist. "I'm okay."

"I can't lose you, Hadley. You're the only family I have left."

My stomach knots and pain shoots through my chest. Five years ago, Brie lost her mom, and two years ago, she lost her dad. She's not close with anyone else in her family. For her, it's only Kenyon and me, and for me, it's only the two of them.

"You're not going to lose me," I whisper, and her arms tighten.

"I can't."

"You won't." I give her a squeeze then let her go when her arms drop away.

"You promise you're okay?"

"I promise," I say, and she studies me for a long moment before pulling in a breath and looking away. "You should go home and wait for Kenyon to get off work."

Her eyes slice back to me. "You know I hate that you always act like everything is fricking hunky-dory when it's not."

"I need a shower," I tell her, not wanting to start another conversation that will have her ranting again. "If you want to hang here while I do that, you know you're more than welcome to. But I'm sure Kenyon would like you to be home when he gets there, and I wouldn't mind at all if you brought me pizza when you come back with him."

"So you're telling me you want me gone." I don't answer. She knows me, knows I like my space and my time alone. Some people feed off others' energy and need it to thrive. Me? I need time to myself and silence to reenergize. "All right," she gives in. "I'll be back with Kenyon and pizza."

"Thank you." I feel my body relax. "I love you."

"I know." She shakes her head then starts to the front door. "Please rest, and if anything—*anything*—happens, call me."

"I will."

"Love you."

My throat burns along with my chest. "I love you too." I give her another hug before she opens the door, and then watch her walk to her car, get in, and back out of my driveway. I scan the street then shut my door and head for my bathroom, where I take a hot shower that does nothing to help me relax.

Hadley

Chapter 2

WITH MY HEAD ON the arm of my couch and my eyes on the TV, I look over my shoulder at the door when someone knocks, and close my eyes, praying the reporters are not back again. A little over an hour after Brie and Kenyon left after bringing pizza and hanging with me for a while, I opened my door to a man I didn't know, with a microphone attached to his hand, and I shut the door in his face. He was the first to knock, but not the last.

The constant ringing of my bell and knocking continued most of the evening, until my landlord and next-door neighbor Tom got home from wherever he spends his days. It stopped after I heard him through the door yelling at the news people. They were parked on the street and standing around on the sidewalk and the lawn, and he told them they were trespassing on private property and if they didn't go away, he'd shoot them. Knowing what I know of Tom from our short acquaintance, I considered that an actual threat, and thankfully, the reporters did too and backed off. I understand why they did; Tom is scary. He's short, maybe five-five, with a stocky build and an ever-present, I'm-not-happy scowl on his face. He's from New Jersey and reminds me of one of the bad guys from the HBO show *The Sopranos*. Actually, I'm pretty sure the only reason he's living here in Tennessee is because he's in the Witness Protection Program for snitching on the mob.

When the knocking comes again and my name is rumbled in a deep voice through the door, I frown and carefully get off the couch. I head around the back of my couch, keeping to the wall and out of sight. Once I'm at the door, I peek out the etched glass at the side, and my heart pounds when I see Cobi standing on my front porch. He looks almost exactly like he did this morning when I woke to find him in my room. His hair is still a little messy, and there is stubble at his jaw, like he didn't get a chance to shave yesterday or today. His eyes still look tired, but he's changed and is now wearing a gray, black, and blue flannel button-down shirt, dark jeans with a cool black belt that his badge is clipped to, and heavy looking boots on his feet.

Crap. What the heck is he doing here?

I jump when he knocks not on the door but on the glass, and I bite my lip hard as he mutters, "Hadley, I can see you. Open the door." I move away from the window to behind the door, hoping to hide myself. Squeezing my eyes closed, I think that maybe, just maybe, he'll think he didn't actually see me if I don't make a noise. "Open the door." He sounds impatient and slightly amused, and my heart lodges in my throat when I open my eyes and see him with his face to the glass and looking at me.

Not wanting to look like a bigger dork, I let out a heavy sigh, unlock the deadbolt, and then turn the handle. As soon as the door opens, he steps into the house and closes the door.

"Hey." I want to roll my eyes at how breathy and desperate I sound, but seriously—he's Cobi freaking Mayson. Every woman in the world would sound breathy and desperate if a man who looked like him stepped into their house.

"Hey." He glances around before his eyes come back to me and travel down the length of my frame. "You going to sleep?"

I glance down at my barely there robe that is covering my nightgown and cringe. "Yes," I lie. I will probably never go to sleep again, not with the vision of Hofstadter dying the way he did playing on a constant loop in my head every time I close my eyes. I think the only reason I was able to get to sleep last night was because the hospital gave me a dose of medication to help me rest. It did the job, and I don't remember anything much after that until I woke up to find Cobi in my room asleep this morning.

"Has the media been here at all since you got home?"

"They showed up this evening," I say. "They left after my landlord, who also happens to be my next-door neighbor, got home and told them to go away." I don't tell him about Tom threatening to shoot them. I don't want him in trouble or want to blow his cover if he is in Witness Protection.

"I should have thought about them showing up here." He shakes his head. "I'm sorry."

"It's not your fault." I shrug before wrapping my arms around my middle. "I'm not sure if you know; I talked to Detective Frank before I left the hospital. I already gave him my statement."

"I know," he says, and I nod then nibble my bottom lip, wondering why he's here if he knows his partner already talked to me. "Wanted to come check on you myself, make sure you're okay."

"I'm okay," I reply quickly, hoping he will feel like his job is done after seeing I'm good and leave.

"All your lights are on," he points out, and I look to where he's looking and see he's not wrong; every light in my place is on, including the little one over the stove.

"What are you doing?" I ask his back as he starts across the room.

"What are you watching?" he asks, not answering my question as he takes a seat on my couch.

I look at the television and point out unnecessarily, "*Cake Boss*."

"Got any beer?"

I blink at him then look around to make sure I haven't somehow found myself in a new dimension. "Beer?"

"Or scotch?"

"Does this look like a bar to you?"

"No." His lips twitch.

"Okay then. No, I don't have beer or scotch."

"Water?"

Oh my God, what the hell is going on?

"Why are you here?"

"I know what you saw last night," he says quietly, and my body gets tight. "I know how going through something like that can fuck with your head."

"I'm fine."

"You're not," he states, still talking quietly. "You don't need to be alone right now."

He's probably right about that, but between being alone and being with him, I choose being alone.

"I'm fine."

"Every light in this place being lit says otherwise." He sits forward, resting his elbows on his knees and testing the boundaries of the shirt he's wearing as his muscles flex. "You wanna talk about it?"

"No," I answer immediately. I don't want to talk about what happened, because I don't want the memories to come back to the surface. I know it's not healthy, but I'm hoping if I don't talk about it or think about what I went through, the memories will just fade away.

"All right, we don't need to talk. We can watch some TV and hang out for a while. When I know you're good, I'll go."

"You don't have to do that. I'm really okay," I say, wondering if he feels obligated to look after me because he's a cop.

"You look about ready to fall over."

My eyes narrow on his. "Are you telling me I look like crap?"

"You're beautiful, darlin'. Still, you look tired," he tells me gently, and my stomach knots at the word beautiful. "Come sit down."

I glance at my couch that is not very big but looks even smaller with him sitting in the middle of it. "You're sitting in the middle," I tell him.

He gives me a strange grin then moves over to the cushion, next to the arm. "Better?"

No, it's not, since he's still sitting on my couch and still in my house, where I have to look at him. My couch could be big enough to fit an entire football team and it still wouldn't be big enough.

Understanding he's not going to leave, I go to the fridge and grab two bottles of water before going back to the couch, and then hand him one as I take a seat. "I'm really okay to be on my own."

"Sure you are," he agrees, like he knows I'm lying.

I don't respond. I pull my legs up under me and stare at the television, trying to ignore the fact that Cobi Mayson is sitting on my couch, something that is really flipping hard to do. His presence feels like it's suffocating me, his masculine scent even from a few feet away, assaulting me and making me want to lean closer to dissect it.

"Your car is in police impound." At his words, I turn to look at him. "There are a few dents, but nothing major. It's still drivable. I'd have brought it back to you myself, but you have to be the one to sign it out." He would have brought it to me? Why would he do that? Just like, why did he send clothes for me to leave the hospital in, and why is he here now? "You can pick it up anytime."

"I'll pick it up tomorrow."

"You got a ride to get it, or do you need one?"

"I have a ride," I say, knowing Brie who I also work with will be more than willing to pick me up in the morning for work and then I can take a cab to get it in the afternoon. "Thanks for letting me know about it. I spaced that I didn't even have it here."

"No problem, and I get that. You've got a lot on your mind. I'm sure you would have remembered sooner or later."

"Yeah, like tomorrow when I was walking out of the house to go to work, which would have been too late to remember," I say jokingly.

He stares at me with a strange look in his eyes, then rumbles, "You're going to work tomorrow?"

"Yes." I frown at his tone.

"Do you think that's smart?"

"Since I have bills to pay, I think it is," I respond, and his jaw clenches.

"I think you need to take a couple days before you get back to work."

"And like I told you earlier, I'm fine."

"Hadley, you were in the hospital last night with a concussion. You got stitches in your forehead and bruising that I can't see but know is there just by the way you're holding yourself. You need to take a couple days to recover before you go back to work."

"Since it's me who was in the hospital, and me who has bruising,

I'm the one who knows what I am and am not capable of, and I'm going back to work tomorrow."

"Are you always so fucking stubborn?"

Yes.

"Fuck, you *are* always this stubborn. You don't even have to say it for me to know."

"You don't know me, Cobi," I point out, and his eyes darken when his name leaves my mouth, that darkness making a few parts of me light up in a way they never have before.

"I will."

What the hell does that mean?

"I need to go to bed." I stand, grabbing the remote and turning the TV off. "Thanks for coming to check on me."

"Hadley." I walk toward the door then look at him when he says my name. "Stop, I'll be cool. Just come sit down."

"I'm tired." It's not a lie; I'm exhausted. I just don't know that I will be able to fall asleep when I get into bed. "I'm going to bed. I appreciate you coming, but you can go now."

"Come sit down." It's an order, and that sets my teeth on edge.

"Goodnight, Cobi." I place my hand on the doorknob and start to turn it.

"I'm not leaving, Hadley. You might be too stubborn to admit you don't want to be alone, but I know you don't want to be. Not right now. Not after what happened last night."

"I'm not stubborn."

"You are."

"I'm not."

He smirks. "Come sit down."

"You need to leave." I open the door, but he still doesn't move; his muscles don't even twitch as he stares at me.

"I'm not leaving, baby, and although you look adorable in that robe, I doubt you want the image of you in it to be all over the news tomorrow," he points out. I look outside then slam the door when I see there are two news vans parked on the street. God, I really hope they didn't see me in what I'm wearing. I hear Cobi laugh, and my teeth grind together as I glare at him. "Come sit down."

"Is it normal for a police officer to show up at someone's house and then refuse to leave when they are asked to… repeatedly?"

"You don't really want me to leave, Hadley."

"You're wrong, Cobi Mayson. I really do want you to leave."

"How do you know me?"

For some reason, that question makes my pulse beat so hard that I feel it in my throat. "What?"

"How do you know me?"

"I don't know you." It's not a lie; I don't know him. Even when we were in school together, I didn't know him—I just knew *of* him.

"Why are you lying?" He frowns, and I let out an annoyed breath. If he thinks I'm stubborn, he should look in the mirror.

"We went to school together."

"We did?" His frown deepens as his eyes roam over my face and hair like he's trying to place me.

"I was a freshman when you were a senior. We didn't know each other. We didn't even have any classes together. I knew of you, because *everyone* knew of you."

"I see, though I can't believe I don't remember you. Even if you were a freshman when I was a senior, there's no way I'd forget a face like yours."

His words are sweet, but he has no idea the girl I was back then. I was not just chubby; I was about sixty pounds overweight. I had acne, glasses that were three sizes too big for my face, and my hair was crazy. I was a nerd. I still am a nerd, but now I'm just a nerd on the inside.

I was teased all the time when I was in school, and I only ever had one friend—that person being Brie. I don't know how or why Brie befriended me way back in fifth grade, but she did, and we stayed tight, even though she could have easily been in the popular crowd. At the beginning of our friendship, I thought she was nice to me because she felt sorry for me, but with time, I learned that was just Brie. She's nice to everyone, she doesn't judge, she doesn't make assumptions, and she never thinks she knows someone's story just from hearsay.

"I don't look like I did back then," I tell him when I notice he hasn't taken his eyes off me. "At all."

"Were you one of those kids who walked around in baggy clothes and all black all the time?"

"No, I was one of the girls who was overweight and awkward. Believe me, if you saw me in the hall, you wouldn't have given me a second glance."

"I doubt that," he mumbles. "I bet you were beautiful even then."

He's so wrong, but I don't think without proof he will believe me. Also him seeing the mess I was back then might scare him into leaving.

"Be right back." I go to my spare bedroom and open the closet. I pull out one of the large plastic totes I have stored there then dig through it until I find what I'm looking for. I take it with me to the living room, sit down in the middle of the couch right next to Cobi, and open the yearbook in my lap. When I find my photo, I point at myself, thinking I'm glad the media chose to use my old Facebook photo instead of the one I'm looking at.

My hair is more frizz than curl. My purple plastic glasses take up half my face and make my nose look scrunched at the end from the weight of them. I'm smiling a weird smile that shows off my crooked teeth, and my cheeks are dotted with acne. Looking at the picture, I know that if I didn't have Brie, I wouldn't have made it out of school unscathed. Kids can be mean, and they were sometimes mean to me, but having Brie and her unwavering friendship, I never felt alone. I always had someone to sit with, someone to hang with, and she never made me feel like I didn't belong.

"You were cute." My head flies around to look at him, and I study his expression to see if he's lying. "You were," he says like he knows what I'm thinking. "Do you still wear glasses?"

"No, I had Lasik surgery a few years ago."

"Bummer, those glasses were cute on you." He taps my picture.

"Are you messing with me right now?" I narrow my eyes on his.

He tips his head to the side. "Messing with you?"

"I don't know. I'm trying to figure out what the heck is going on. You being nice, sending clothes for me, and then showing up here and demanding to hang out to make sure I'm okay."

"Not sure you're ready for that much honesty."

Okay, what does that mean? I don't ask. Part of me doesn't want to know. Really, I don't think I could handle his honesty right now. "Maybe we should just watch some TV," I mumble.

His eyes turn knowing and he smiles. "Good idea, baby."

I don't say anything more. I set the yearbook down, pick up the remote, and turn the TV back on. I flip through channels for something to watch and end up stopping on a show about treasure hunters. We sit in silence through two episodes, and never, not once, do the guys looking for treasure ever find anything more than some old pottery. Still, I can't seem to stop hoping they'll find what they're looking for. When the third episode starts, my eyes get heavy, but I force myself to keep them open, not trusting that I will be able to keep the memories at bay if I fall asleep.

"Hadley." At my name, I look at Cobi and see his expression is soft and filled with understanding. "You're safe. Lay down and close your eyes. I won't let anything happen to you."

"I—"

"Promise," he cuts me off. "You're safe with me."

Safe with him.

Lord, Cobi Mayson is seriously sweet—and seriously observant. I lick my lips, and without a word, I lie down, resting my head against the arm of the couch. I tuck my legs up close to my chest so my feet don't touch him, then let out a breath when he pulls the blanket from the back of the couch and places it over me. My eyes start to feel funny, like I might cry, but I refuse to give in to the feeling. I lie there for a long time, not expecting to fall asleep, but apparently I do.

And with Cobi looking after me, I sleep peacefully.

Hadley — Cobi

Hadley

Chapter 3

"TIME'S UP." AT BRIE'S statement, my eyes go from the paperwork I'm filling out to her. I watch her shut the door to my office then walk across the carpet and take a seat in the chair across from mine. She pauses, running her hands down the top of her pants before looking at me. "We need to talk about Cobi Mayson."

At the mention of Cobi, my heart starts to beat oddly and my stomach drops. When I woke up this morning, Cobi wasn't sitting on my couch a few inches away, where he was last night when I fell asleep. At some point, he maneuvered us so that I was tucked tightly against his chest with his strong arm around my waist, holding me securely against him so I wouldn't fall off the couch. I came awake to the feel of him around me and his breath whispering against my neck.

I knew then that I couldn't handle what was happening, so I did what any sane girl would do. I pretended nothing happened at all. I quickly and carefully got away from him, stood up, and started getting ready for work. I expected him to be gone when I got out of the shower or to still be asleep, but instead, he was in my kitchen making me coffee and breakfast, as if he had done it a million times. He was also still there when Brie showed up to take me to work, and even though she didn't ask and he didn't say much, I knew she was curious as to why he was at my place so early.

"Cobi?" I try my hand at playing dumb, but her eyes narrow on mine.

"Cobi Mayson, who was at your house this morning."

"Oh, that?" I wave my hand out in front of me. "That was nothing. He's just being nice."

"Did he stay with you last night?" I start to open my mouth, but before I can make up a fib, she continues. "And don't lie. I know when you're lying to me."

I chew on my bottom lip, something that is a horrible habit of mine, and then mutter, "He slept on the couch."

"He slept on your couch?"

"Well…" I pause, trying to come up with something to say, and then figure a half-truth will soothe her. "I think he knew I would have a hard time sleeping if I was alone." I don't feel guilty for leaving out the fact that I also slept on the couch, that I'm pretty sure I slept better than I have in months, maybe years, and that I woke up with him holding me.

"You could have had me or Kenyon there, or like I said yesterday, you could have stayed with us."

"I didn't exactly invite him over, Brie. He showed up and kind of refused to leave, even when I asked him to go a few dozen times."

She blinks at me. "What?"

"Like I said, he's being nice."

"Right, and this morning when I got there, he was in your kitchen cleaning up what looked like breakfast dishes."

"He was hungry." My stomach flutters like it did this morning when I came out of my bedroom to eggs, toast, and coffee, and him waiting for me.

"Exactly how hard did you hit your head?"

"My head is fine." I roll my eyes.

"Okay, so then tell me the truth about you and Cobi."

"There is nothing to tell you."

"Honey—" She sits forward in her chair, her voice dropping like she's talking to a small child. "—a man does not sit guard over a woman he is not interested in, or make her breakfast."

34

"He's just being nice. He's a cop." I shrug. "It's his job to look after people."

"I'm sure." She rolls her eyes. "Or you're totally oblivious and not seeing the fact that he wants you in a bad way."

"I'm not interested," I lie. I totally *am* interested, but there is no way I'd go there—not with him. Him being a cop is just icing on the cake. If he knew my family's history, he would… well, I don't know what he would do. But there is no way I would subject him to my family or my past.

She shakes her head, her long hair bouncing across her shoulders. "I don't think he cares if you are or if you aren't interested. Really, I don't think he's the kind of man who understands the word no."

"Can we stop talking about this? There is really nothing going on between him and me, and we need to work."

"He wants you."

"Brie," I sigh.

She shakes her head again. "He's Cobi Mayson, Hadley. Every girl in school crushed on him, and I saw him yesterday and this morning. I have no doubt that every woman who he crosses paths with crushes on him now. He's gorgeous and you're you. You're beautiful, a little bit of a pain in the ass, but sweet. I'm sure he's seeing all that is you and thinking he wants in there."

"I think you're overthinking this whole thing." I grab my purse from the drawer in my desk and stand. "I have to go. I need to take a cab to pick up my car then I need to get to the Shelps' for their home study." I walk around my desk.

"Fine." She gets up from her chair but stops me, wrapping her hand around my arm before I can make it to the door. "If he is interested, will you please give him a chance?"

Even though it's never going to happen, I nod.

"You deserve good things in your life, Hadley."

"I have good things in my life," I respond instantly, and then continue quietly. "I have you and Kenyon, and a job I love doing. I'm happy, so please stop thinking I'm not."

Her eyes search mine before going soft. "You could be happier."

She might be right, but I learned at a very early age to never put my trust in a man, and to never expect a man to be the one to make me happy. I don't want to be so cynical, but I gave up on the opposite sex a long time ago. I'm twenty-eight years old, and the only guy I have ever really trusted is Kenyon. It took me years to get to that point with him, because all the other men I know have been druggies, liars, and cheaters. My dad, the first man to ever be a fixture in my life, was all three of those things.

"I love you and totally understand that you want good things for me, but I really can't talk about this right now. I need to go."

"Tonight, dinner with me and Kenyon. We'll talk about it then."

"Brie—"

"Hadley, I'm worried about you," she whispers, sliding her hand down my arm, taking my hand, and giving it a squeeze. "You just went through something traumatic, and like always, you're pretending like nothing happened, like nothing has changed. As your best friend, I need to know you're really okay. Please give me that."

I swallow and bite my bottom lip before nodding. I know she worries about me; she always has. She just doesn't understand that sometimes it's easier to pretend like everything is perfect than to acknowledge how messed up things really are. I don't like going into the past. I don't want to relive everything I have been through, because at the end of the day it's a waste of time to constantly look back. And I know firsthand that it takes more courage to keep moving forward.

"I'll see you tonight," she says, and I nod once more.

I hurry out of my office, out of the building, and call a cab. When I get my car, it's just like Cobi said—dented up but still drivable. Thank God.

"You fucking bitch. You think you can fucking judge me? You think you can come in here and from a five-minute look around decide it's the right thing to do to take my kids away from me?"

"Mr. Shelp, please calm down," I urge softly, keeping my distance from the man who is standing a few feet away in the open door to his home. "If you clean things up, and—"

"Fuck you," he cuts me off, pointing at me, my words doing nothing but pissing him off more. "You're going to get what's coming to you, bitch. Be prepared. You took something from me, so I'm going to take something from you." He walks into his house, slamming the door. I close my eyes for a moment, pulling in a deep breath before getting into my car, which is parked on the street.

I sit, staring at the house, but not really seeing it at all, because tears fill my eyes, making it blurry. This is the part of my job I hate, the part I wish I didn't have to do. I always knew from the time I was young that I wanted to be a social worker. I didn't know exactly what the job entailed; I just knew I wanted to be a voice for the kids who were too young to speak up for themselves. Growing up the child of two people who were more concerned with getting drunk or high than me, I needed someone to step in for me, but no one ever did. No one ever cared that my parents spent all their money on drugs and booze. Not one person took a second to make sure I had food in my stomach or a safe place to rest my head at night.

I don't know how my life would have turned out if someone did care enough to make a call to social services to let them know they had concerns about my well-being. All I know is that now, I'm the person who has to go into people's homes to check on children those around them have concerns about. Children like Mr. Shelp's ten-year-old daughter Lisa and twelve-year-old son Eric, whose school called wanting to make sure the kids were okay when they were at home with their father. The report we received told us that both kids regularly showed up at school in dirty clothes, often telling their teachers they hadn't eaten or that their dad hadn't been around in days.

Even with the information provided to me in that first report, I didn't make any assumptions. I know better than to go into a situation assuming the worst. Things happen. Life happens. People have bad days or bad weeks, and families often struggle to put food on the table. I, for one, never want to be the reason a child is taken from the only home they know, the only people they know, without having a valid reason.

During my first visit to the Shelps, I saw for myself that the school's concerns were valid. Mr. Shelp greeted me at the door drunk then led me into his home, which was a wreck. The place wasn't just "lived in." It was unlivable. There were dirty dishes everywhere, along with open alcohol containers, full ashtrays, used condoms, and trash… so much trash. The floors were covered in a thick layer of garbage, including the kids' bedroom. Worse, there was no edible food in the cupboards or fridge.

It was during the first visit when I made a decision that both kids should be removed from the home until things were cleaned up, and only then would their situation be reevaluated. Today was my second home study. I expected to come and find things better than they were the last time I was here. Unfortunately, I found that nothing had changed, including Mr. Shelp, who was wasted yet again.

Once I get myself under control and know I will be able to drive without endangering anyone, I pull out onto the street and head back to the office to fill out the necessary paperwork. Both Mr. Shelp's children have been placed with a local family for the time being, and I know from working with their foster family in the past that they are being well taken care of.

Sadly, some foster families are in it for the money. Those are usually the ones people hear about on the news or through the grapevine, but there are families who just want to help. Families like the McKays, who have never been able to have children of their own and have thrived off being able to take in kids who need a soft place to fall when life is rocky. The McKays have now adopted ten kids, and three of them are currently in college. They've also had countless foster kids stay with them over the years, and most children don't want to leave when it's time for them to return to their biological parents. I wish more foster parents were like them.

Unfortunately, being a foster parent is not easy and is often a double-edged sword. When you sign up to foster, you know what your role is. You know you will likely have to give the child back to his or her biological parent or parents, but attachments happen and feelings get involved, making it difficult.

I have never done it, but I can't imagine loving a child after knowing their history and their story, and then having to let them return to a situation that might not be the healthiest for them. Still, the courts believe kids should be with their biological parents and that we, as social workers, should work toward that, no matter what, which means often times kids are taken from people who could provide for them and returned to their parents who are just that—their parents.

Not all situations that come across my desk are the same. I have, over the years, had more than a few adoptive families who just need me to help them with finalizing their adoptions, or families who've had calls placed against them that have been inaccurate. I can't even tell you how many times I've had to investigate a family because someone made a false claim against them out of spite.

When I reach the office, I see Marian's car is the only one left in the lot, meaning all my co-workers are out. *Great.* I park, then head inside the building and rush toward my office. I don't even stop in the staff kitchen for the cup of coffee I desperately need, because I don't want to run into my boss. It's not nice, but I try to avoid Marian as much as possible. She rubs me the wrong way. She's judgmental and arrogant and always talking down to anyone and everyone, including the families she's supposed to be helping. How or why she became a social worker, I do not know. What I do know is that she would better serve as a warden for a prison.

When I reach my office door, I grind to a halt and stare at Marian sitting at my desk, looking at my computer.

"Is everything okay?"

At my question, her head flies up and surprise fills her eyes before she wipes the look away and attempts to frown, the Botox she's had done making it difficult.

"Why wouldn't everything be okay?"

"I don't know." I move into my office, and when I start toward my desk, I see she has some forms pulled up on my computer. I try to get a look at what she's doing, but she quickly exits whatever it is she's looking at.

Okay, what the hell is going on?

"I needed to use your computer. Mine isn't working."

I study her for a long time, trying to gauge if she's lying or not, but I can't read her. Really, I have no reason to think she would lie about her computer not working, since our systems haven't been updated in years and my computer just went out a week ago.

"Did you get what you needed?" I set my purse on the edge of my desk and her eyes move to it.

"When did you get that bag?" I look at my Coach purse, a gift I bought myself for my birthday—a gift that didn't cost even half as much as it should have, since I got it at the outlet store in Nashville.

"A few weeks ago."

"How could you afford it?" At her question, I'm physically reminded of how much I don't like her when I feel the muscles around my spine get tight.

"Pardon?"

"I'm only asking, because we've had some discrepancies come up over the last few months."

"Discrepancies?"

"Some of the funds that have been allotted to a few of the kids for things they needed have gone missing."

"What?" My stomach rolls at the idea of someone taking from the kids, kids who don't have much to begin with, who count on the little we give them.

"Never mind. It's not something you need to worry about." She stands from my chair and walks around me toward the door. "I'm looking into things."

"How much has been taken?"

At my question, she turns to look at me. "I can't tell you that information. Just know that when I find out who took that money, they will be answering to me before they do some major jail time."

"Why am I just hearing about this?" I question out loud. Marian is my boss, but I am still a part of management. I should have heard about this; I should know about missing funds.

"We don't want anyone to know. Right now, everyone is a suspect." I feel my eyes narrow, and seeing my look, she continues, "Scott knows.

I informed him about the missing funds and he asked me to keep it quiet while the situation is being investigated."

"Do you have any suspects?"

"Everyone is a suspect," she repeats, and I feel my muscles tense. I have worked with everyone at this agency for over five years. I trust each and every one of them. I know most of their families and friends and their histories. It's not easy for me to believe that one of them would do something so horrible. "You cannot speak about this," she says, her face going hard. "What I just told you is confidential. I shouldn't even have mentioned it to you."

"I won't say anything," I agree, and she nods once before leaving my office and heading across the open floor space. I keep watching until she closes her office door.

I go to my desk and take a seat, my mind spinning as I attempt to come up with a plausible explanation for the missing funds. Each month, we are allotted monies for kids in the system, monies that are used to pay for extra things, like sports uniforms, musical instruments, and such. That money is always accounted for; we have to write a report and explain in detail why we are using those funds. If money is missing, there has to be a paper trail. No funds are ever given out without written approval and the proper paperwork being filed. Not having a clue of what to do about that, I do what needs to get done.

I use my mouse and bring my computer back to life then type up the report for the Shelps' file, after I finish with that, I call the McKays and inform them that both Shelp children will be with them until further notice. Mrs. McKay, who has been through this before, is understanding and promises to speak with both kids when they get home from school. She also tells me that since the kids have been staying with her and her husband, their grades have already improved. I'm not surprised; a loving environment, eating regularly, and having good people around tends to bring the best out of kids, even when they are going through a traumatic experience.

Before I get off the phone with Mrs. McKay, I set up another visit so I can see the kids for myself just to make sure they are adjusting to their new living situation. By the time I get off the phone and close down my computer, it's after five. I saw Brie come into the office not long ago and know she will be shutting things down to head home soon too, so I gather my stuff and head toward her cubical in the center of the room. I see she's on the phone, so I don't approach, but she lifts her head and smiles at me, giving me a five-minute signal. I nod and head toward the kitchen, hoping to get a cup of coffee before it's dumped down the drain.

I'm just in time. I get the last cup then spend a few minutes cleaning up the kitchen before meeting Brie. She tells me that she's made us reservations at one of my favorite restaurants, a local Greek place that doesn't only have the best fresh oysters around, but a Gyro plate that even thinking about makes my mouth water. After I agree to meet her at the restaurant at seven, we part ways and I head home.

Today has been surprisingly quiet. Not that my cell phone hasn't been ringing every five minutes from unknown callers, but no reporters showed up at my job—something I was honestly worried about happening. Even my co-workers who know what happened have been quiet. Yes, they asked if I was all right or needed anything, but they didn't badger me for information or question me excessively, which was a relief.

When I get home, I head right for my bedroom and change out of my heels, slacks, and button-down top I wore to work. I put on a pair of dark skinny jeans and a wraparound silver-gray sweater, just in case we eat outside on the patio, which is something we do often, and slip on my flats. When I'm finished getting ready, I stop in my kitchen to grab a bottle of water from the fridge but pause when I see a note on my kitchen counter. The handwriting is neat but masculine. The words written are short and to the point.

I'll be back tonight
It will probably be late
Cobi

My heart feels heavy in my chest as I pick up the note and read it again. I close my eyes and lean my head back against my shoulders, trying to figure out how I can feel relief and fear at the exact same time. Without an answer, I set the note back down, grab my bottle of water then my keys and purse, and leave.

One thing I know for sure—nothing can ever happen between Cobi and me, even if I want *everything* to happen between us.

Chapter 4

"WE LOVE YOU, HADLEY," Kenyon says when we reach my car, and my fingers wrap tighter around my keys. There is always a little pain involved when I hear those words, pain because as much as I want to believe that I understand the emotion of love, I don't think I do. Not really anyway.

I look way up. At six foot seven, Kenyon doesn't just tower over me; he towers over everyone. Even Brie, who is six feet tall and always wears at least three-inch heels, has to tip her head way back to look up at her man. That's one of the reasons she told me she fell in love with him. Most men she'd dated were her height, or not much taller, so she never got to wear heels, and the men never made her feel feminine or dainty. Kenyon could make some of the biggest men I know feel feminine and dainty, with his giant size and presence. He's a mechanic; he's rough around the edges, and could probably crush someone with one flick of his wrist, though I doubt he'd ever do that. He's too nice, probably one of the nicest people I have ever met. "We're just concerned about you."

"I know." I lean into him when he wraps his arms around me, and my gaze locks with Brie's, who is standing close to us, when I see her eyes start to fill with tears. Once more, I swallow hard and whisper, "Just a couple more days, and then I promise I'll talk to whoever you want me to talk to."

"Swear?" Brie moves in closer, holding out her pinky, and I step away from Kenyon and wrap my pinky around hers before our thumbs press together.

"Swear." With our hands still locked together, I wrap my arm around her.

"Are you sure we can't talk you into staying with us, just for a few days?"

I smile and lean back to look at her. "No."

"Fine." She rolls her eyes then Kenyon's arm wraps around my shoulders, squeezing me into his side before he lets me go and grabs Brie's hand. "Are we still on for tomorrow?"

"When have I ever missed one of our Saturdays?" I ask back. For years, once a month, we go get our nails done, have lunch, and go see a movie. It's our day.

"True. I'll be at your place at ten to pick you up."

"Eleven," Kenyon states, and Brie tips her head back toward him.

When she reads the look on his face, she smiles then looks at me. "Eleven," she says, and I giggle.

I open the door to my car and slide in behind the wheel. "See you tomorrow."

"Call when you get home."

"I will."

"Also, tomorrow, we are going to have a serious talk about Cobi," she says over her shoulder as Kenyon starts to lead her away.

"Great," I mumble, and she laughs. At dinner, she brought Cobi up more than once. She also watched me closely, and looked at me like I was lying every time I told her I'm not interested in him.

I slam my door and watch through my front window as Kenyon walks her to his SUV and helps her in before going around to the driver's side. They don't pull out of the parking lot until I do, and I hear their horn honk as we take off in opposite directions.

When I make it home, I notice the street is empty, no news vans or media outlets in sight. Maybe the story of what happened is already old news, or maybe the media realized I had nothing to do with what happened to Harmony while she was working at the hospital.

I grab my mail from the box at the end of the driveway then glance to the left to see Tom standing on his front porch smoking a cigarette. Seriously, he has to be a mobster. What other kind of guy wears tracksuits when they are hanging at home? I give him a wave when our eyes meet, not surprised when he doesn't wave back, but his chin does lift in greeting. With a shake of my head, I walk into my house, turning on all the lights as I go. I drop the mail and my purse on the island, then head to my bedroom and change into one of my nightgowns, throwing my robe over it. I wash my face, then settle on the couch to watch some TV for a couple hours before going to bed.

With tired eyes, I watch the time on my alarm clock change from 12:59 to 1:00 a.m. I've been lying in bed, sleep evading me for almost four hours now. Or maybe it's me who is avoiding sleep? I wish I could say I haven't been waiting up for Cobi, but the truth is I have been.

I pull my blanket up over my head, realizing how quiet my house is. It's not lonely, just quiet. I had a cat for a few years; I adopted her from the Humane Society when I rented my first apartment my junior year of college. Her name was Shy. She was old and needed daily medication, but she was also sweet, even-tempered, loved to cuddle, and never acted out. Right after I adopted her, I took her to the vet for a checkup, and they told me they didn't think she'd live longer than two years. They were right, but those two years were good ones, not only for her but for me too.

I miss her now more than ever. Having another living, breathing being around made the quiet not so loud. Maybe tomorrow I'll check out my lease and see if it says anything about having a pet. If it says pets are okay with a deposit, I'll talk to Tom.

I've never had a dog. I'm not even sure I could handle the responsibility of having a dog, but I will totally be looking at dogs. Maybe one of those cute tiny ones I can carry around with me everywhere I go. I smile at the thought then jump when I hear my doorbell ring.

My heart starts to race and my body starts to feel like it's filled with electricity at the idea of Cobi being at my door. When the bell goes off again, I toss my blankets off me, grab my robe from the end of my bed, and head through my still lit living room toward the front door, tying the belt around my waist as I go. When I see Cobi is watching me move closer through the glass at the side of my door, my stomach fills with butterflies. I don't hesitate to unlock the locks and turn the handle, and he doesn't hesitate to walk right inside my house and close the door. Seriously, he's handsome. Just like yesterday, he has on boots and jeans, with his badge clipped to his belt. Unlike yesterday, he's wearing a button down, black fitted shirt tucked into his jeans, a shirt that is molded to his frame, showing everyone with eyes just how the style of shirt he's wearing is supposed to fit.

"You're in your bed, yet you still got all the lights on out here," he says while looking around, and I start to open my mouth, but before I can respond, he continues. "Baby, the only way you're going to be able to deal with what happened is to talk about it. Being stubborn isn't going to fix things."

"Pardon?" I stand a little taller so I don't feel so intimidated with him towering over me and looking down at me.

"You're being stubborn."

"I'm fine," I snap, leaving out the fact that Brie and Kenyon have already convinced me that I need to talk to someone, and that I have agreed to do so.

"Sweetheart, you're scared of sleeping in your own home. You're not fine."

My eyes narrow on his in annoyance. "You don't know me."

"No, not completely, but I do know you're being stubborn about this."

"For your information, I've never liked sleeping in the dark."

I have never been able to sleep when a room is pitch black. I have always needed a little bit of light, which is why most of the time I have my sound machine on that also gives off a soft blue glow that doesn't keep me awake but does give me just enough light to see the room around me.

"Never?" he asks quietly while his eyes scan mine. Eyes that seem to see everything, even the things I don't want him to see.

"Never." I give him a shrug then lie. "And I was almost asleep when you rang my door bell."

His lips twitch. "You're so full of shit."

"What?"

"You're full of shit, babe. Saw you last night right before you conked out. Remember exactly how your eyes and face looked then. You were not falling asleep when I rang the bell. You might have been tryin' to, but you weren't even close to getting there."

He remembers how my eyes and face looked before I fell asleep?

No, no. I shake my head. I will not let his words make me feel giddy.

"Has anyone ever told you that you are really fricking annoying?"

"A time or two."

"I bet." I rest my hands on my hips and glare at him.

"So do you wanna hang on the couch with me and watch some TV, or you wanna go to bed and try to get some sleep?"

"So you're saying you're not leaving." I pause then add, "Again, even though I'm telling you that you don't have to be here and I'm fine."

"I'm not leaving," he confirms.

"Is this a new service officers are providing for the citizens of this county?"

"No." His eyes lock on mine and fill with something I don't understand. "This is a service I'm providing exclusively to you."

"Why?"

"Like I said before." His voice drops before he continues, "I'm not sure you're ready for that much honesty."

Looking into his eyes, I know he's right. No way in hell am I ready for his kind of honesty. "I'm going to bed."

"Figured." He grins and my nipples tingle. Seriously, he has great eyes, great hair, and a great body, but his mouth and his grin are over-the-top sexy. I'm sure Brie is right about every woman he comes in contact with crushing on him.

Unwilling to think about why that makes my stomach churn with unease, I turn on my bare feet, lean over the back of the couch, and grab the remote. I turn on the television then toss the remote in his direction. I don't hear it hit the floor, so I know he catches it.

I don't look at him again or say anything more before leaving him in my living room and heading for my bedroom. One, because I'm pretty sure whatever I'd say would come out a complete mess, making me look like a tool. Two, because I don't want to acknowledge how thankful I am that he's here… again. And even though I will never admit it, I feel more at ease with him in my house. And three, if I did acknowledge why he's here, I would want to find some not-so-very ladylike ways to thank him for what he's doing. Those things would include kissing him, probably groping him, and maybe—if I was lucky—each of us orgasming.

I shut the door to my room and get into bed. I don't even have a chance to really think about Cobi being in my house, because I fall asleep almost as soon as my head hits my pillow.

No.

Oh God, no.

Fear fills the pit of my stomach then rushes through me when I see the gun in his hands. He doesn't say a word, but the dark look in his cold eyes says it all—he's going to kill me.

My limbs tremble and a shiver slides down my spine.

I want to move. I want to run. But I'm frozen in place.

My eyes close.

This is the end.

Bang!

I scream, waiting to feel the pain I know is coming.

"Baby." Arms wrap around me and I fight against their hold, needing to run, needing to get away now that I'm not frozen in place. "Calm down. You're safe. Promise you're safe."

"Co… bi?" His name comes out ragged as my lungs fight to fill with oxygen.

"Breathe, you're safe. Home," he tells me. I try. I try so hard, but I can't seem to get enough air into my lungs. I can't seem to catch my breath. My chest hurts, and my lungs feel like they might explode. "Come on." I'm pulled to sit on the side of the bed then I feel his hand on my back, pressing down and forcing my head between my legs. "Breathe, baby, just breathe. You're home."

Home… I'm home. I'm not in the middle of the woods, running for my life, not lying helpless on the ground and staring at the gun I know will kill me. One short sharp breath after another comes until eventually my lungs fill with the oxygen I need to breathe easily.

Tears fill my eyes as Cobi's hand rubs soothing circles on my back, his softly spoken words of encouragement telling me to breathe, telling me that I'm okay, and pull me back to reality. I lift my head, and his hand slides around my neck and his thumb presses into my jaw.

"I'm sorry." Tears leak down my cheeks, and with the blue light in my room, I see his face soften then watch in fascination as it comes closer to mine.

His warm, soft lips touch my forehead and my eyes slide closed. "You have nothing to apologize for."

"I—"

"You need to talk to someone, Hadley. You need to talk to someone so you can work this out of you."

"I know." I drop my forehead, but he doesn't move back, so it ends up resting against his chin. "I already agreed to talk to someone. Brie is going to make me an appointment with someone she knows."

His movements still for a moment, before he whispers, "Good." His hand skims down my back and his chin slides to the side so that his cheek is resting against the crown of my head. "It will get easier once you talk about it."

I nod, and my hands ball into fists. When I realize his shirt is bunched between my fingertips, I quickly let my hands drop to my sides. "I'm… I'm so sorry about that."

"Don't be. I'm just glad I was here." He leans away, and I tip my head back to look up at him. "You need some water?"

"Yeah. Please." I also need a moment away from him, away from the way he makes me feel. I should not be clinging to a man I do not know. I should not be thinking about how thankful I am that he's here right now. How safe I feel in his presence.

"Be right back."

My breath catches in my throat when he leans in, pressing a soft kiss to my forehead, and my eyes slide closed and don't open again until I hear him leave my bedroom. I don't lie down; I scoot to the middle of my bed and rest with my back to my headboard, bringing my blankets up to my chest. When Cobi comes back in, I notice his hair is rumpled and his eyes are tired. I also see his boots are off and his shirt is untucked with his sleeves rolled up to his elbows. I glance at the clock on my bedside table; it's after four in the morning.

"Were you asleep?"

"What?"

"I...." I shake my head. "Did you sleep on my couch?" I ask, as he comes toward me, holding one of my glasses filled with water.

"Yeah, passed out not too long after you went to bed."

Crap, I suck. Here I am sleeping in my nice, warm comfortable bed, and I didn't even offer him a pillow or a blanket.

I take the glass of water from him, have a sip, and then close my eyes and sigh. "I'm a jerk."

"Excuse me?" The bed dips as he takes a seat on it next to my outstretched legs.

"You've been nice, and I didn't even offer to get you a pillow."

His hand rests on the top of my foot, and just that simple contact makes butterflies take flight in my stomach once more. "I've slept in worse places with a whole lot less. Trust me, I'm good."

I want to ask what he means, where he's slept that's been worse, but I don't. When I notice he's fighting a grin, I frown and ask, "What?"

"You're worried about my well-being."

Rolling my eyes, I fight back a smile. "Maybe you're not annoying. Maybe you're just cocky."

I watch him throw back his head and laugh, and the sound washes over me, making me feel triumphant. When he stops laughing and his eyes meet mine, my breath catches in my throat. I don't know what it is I see in his dark gaze, but I do know it makes me feel like I should either run away as fast as I can, or hold on as tightly as possible. "Hadley." His eyes search mine as he leans in closer to me. "You okay to go back to sleep?"

At the thought of lying in the dark alone, fear starts to weave its way through my system like the intricate details of a spider's web, but instead of saying no, I nod while whispering, "Yeah."

"Liar." His thumb slides across my cheek. "You're a pretty liar, but you're still a liar."

"I'm not a liar," I state, as he takes the water cup from my hand and sets it on my bedside table.

"You are, but I figure with time that will change, but even if it doesn't, I'll learn to read you."

He stands, and my heart races, thinking he's going to leave. But then blood starts to rush through my veins when he takes off his badge and drops it next to my water, and then he pulls out his cell phone and wallet, doing the same with both of them. I open my mouth to ask what he's doing, but shut it when he gets in bed next to me, resting his back against my headboard and shoving his arm behind my shoulders, pulling me closer to him. Every part of me freezes solid when he cups the back of my head and forces my cheek to his hard chest. "Relax, and try to get some sleep."

I almost laugh. Does he honestly expect me to relax while he's not only in my bed but holding me against his muscular body? Relax when his smell is making me dizzy?

"Relax, Hadley. I got you," he says softly, while his fingers slide through my hair. Squeezing my eyes closed, I debate telling him there is no way in hell I'm going to be able to relax with him around, but my muscles start to slowly loosen with his fingers working their magic, the steady beat of his heart against my ear, and his even breathing. "That's it, baby. Sleep," he whispers right before I fall asleep, and once again, I sleep like a baby with Cobi watching over me.

"So you're here again." At that statement from Brie, my eyes slowly blink open. They widen when my vision clears and I see the time on the clock next to my bed.

"Yep," Cobi states, and my heart begins to pound.

"So did you spend the night again?" At Brie's question, I toss back the blanket and roll off the bed, ungracefully. I look like a fish out of water then almost fall on my face.

"Don't answer her!" I shout, pulling open my door and rushing out of my room. I skid to a halt in front of the kitchen island where Brie and Cobi are standing on opposite sides. "Do not answer her. It's a trap."

"A trap?" Brie narrows her eyes on me.

"Yes, a trap." I look at Cobi. "Do not answer her."

"So don't tell her we slept together again?" His lips twitch as his eyes fill with humor.

"Again." Brie raises a brow at me.

"We did not sleep together," I snap.

"We didn't?" Cobi questions, and I turn to glare at him.

"We didn't sleep together."

"We did," he states with a casual shrug while picking up his coffee then taking a sip.

"You slept with him twice?" Brie asks.

"No. Okay, yes, we did *sleep* together, but we didn't actually sleep together. I mean, we *did* actually sleep together." I look at Cobi when he starts to laugh. "This is not funny."

"So you did or you didn't sleep together?" Brie frowns, looking confused.

"Fine!" I toss up my arms. "We didn't have sex; we just slept together."

"That's what I said. We slept together," Cobi says, and Brie starts to laugh.

"If you're both done annoying me, I need to go get ready."

"I also gotta head out," Cobi states, looking at the clock on the microwave. "You mind if I steal your girl for a minute?" he asks Brie.

"Not at all. A minute, a month, forever maybe." She winks at him, and he laughs.

"Come on." I take Cobi's hand and drag him into my room then shut the door. "Can you please stop charming my friend?"

"So now I'm charming?" A growl sounds in my throat and my hands ball into fists as I stare into his humor-filled eyes. "Should I start making a list?"

"Sure," I snap, "and why don't you add *ass* to it?"

"Not sure I like that one." He grins. "Unless you're referring to the quality of my ass."

"Don't you need to leave?" I wave my hand at the door he's standing next to.

"You're the one who hauled me into your bedroom, baby."

"Well then, you can go."

"Can I get a kiss goodbye?" His eyes drop to my mouth, and mine drop to his.

My pulse quickens and my stomach dips. *Yes, all the yesses!* My mind screams, but "Absolutely not" leaves my mouth.

"Absolutely not? That's pretty firm, considering the way you were just looking at my mouth."

My eyes turn to slits. "I was not looking at your mouth."

"Liar."

"She lies all the time!" Brie shouts from the other side of the door, and I groan while Cobi starts to laugh.

"Shut up, Brie, and get away from my door, you spy."

"I dropped an earring," she says, and I roll my eyes toward the ceiling and hold them there, praying to get caught in a vortex that will send me to another time or place.

"What are you doing today?" Cobi asks, and my eyes meet his.

"Just girl stuff then a movie with Brie."

"Good." He reaches out, wrapping his fingers around a piece of my hair before tucking it behind my ear. "What time do you think you'll be home?"

Whenever you say you're going to be here.

"Late, really late."

"She's lying. She'll be home by six," Brie states, sounding like she's smiling.

"Oh my God, get away from my door, Brie."

"Just trying to help a brother out," she mumbles.

"It's appreciated," Cobi calls, and I groan then jerk my eyes to his when he grabs my hand. "I'm off duty today. Gonna help my dad with some stuff. But I'll be here at six with pizza."

"I don't thi—"

"See you then." He brushes his mouth against mine, startling me silent and sending my body into a frenzy. Without another word, he opens the door and leaves me standing in my room frozen in place. I hear him say goodbye to Brie, and then I listen to the front door open and close.

"I really like him," Brie says, dancing into my bedroom, her long hair tied up in a ponytail bouncing with her. "Like a lot, and he's funny." She plops down on my bed, and I turn to look at her, wondering how it's possible that my lips are still tingling—how every inch of me is still tingling. "I didn't expect him to be funny, because he has that whole serious badass vibe about him, but he's really funny."

"Brie." I know she hears my warning when she rolls her eyes.

"Don't tell me to stop or give me the same 'I'm not interested' crap you gave me yesterday, because you and I both know that's a lie."

"Brie."

"Hadley, a woman would have to be dead not to be interested in him, and I'm thinking that even then they'd turn into the walking dead if he were around."

"I need to get ready." I sigh when I see she's not going to give this up anytime soon.

"You do that. I'm going to call Ken and fill him in on what happened."

I stop digging through my drawers and turn to look at her. "Are you serious?"

"Yep." She pulls her phone out, dials, and then puts it to her ear. "Hey, babe, you are not going to believe this."

I don't wait around to listen to her talk to Kenyon. I don't need a recap of this morning. I really don't need to spend any more time thinking about Cobi, who's barely there brush of the lips left me paralyzed—Cobi, who will be back again tonight with pizza.

I get dressed in a pair of my favorite jeans, with a white tank top and a light sweater over it, and then slip on a pair of sandals so I won't mess up my pedicure. I quickly run a brush through my hair, add a little mascara to my lashes, and then swipe some gloss on my lips. When I'm done and come out of the bathroom, I find Brie exactly where I left her, still on the phone and lying on my bed. Her eyes meet mine, and she smiles then says goodbye to Kenyon and hangs up.

"I'm thinking we should go to the wax place before we head to the nail salon," she states as she gets off my bed.

"I'm not getting waxed." I shake my head and head to the kitchen to grab my purse.

"When was the last time you—" She pauses. "You know, took care of things down there?" She stops at the island as I go to the fridge to grab a bottle of water.

"We are not talking about this."

"Just answer this. Can you wear a swimsuit right now without worrying?"

"Seriously?"

"I'm your best friend. If anyone can ask you this kind of thing, it's me."

"My vagina is fine, and I'm not sleeping with anyone, so it doesn't matter anyway."

"You've already slept with Cobi twice. Eventually, one of you is going to push things past just sleeping. You need to be prepared for that when it happens."

A vision of Cobi and me fills my mind, but I push it away.

"Have you always been this insane?"

"Come on, it won't even take but twenty minutes tops, and you have to admit you'll feel better knowing it's done."

"I'm thinking about going natural from now on. Hairy legs, underarms, and bush." Her nose scrunches up. "Can we go now?" I ask.

"Yep." She types something into the phone still in her hand then looks at me. "But I'm driving."

"Fine by me. That means I can drink wine at the theater."

"Crap, I didn't think about that," she mumbles, and I smile. The theater we go to is one of those dine-in ones with fully reclining chairs, dinner, and drinks if you want them. It's awesome.

I follow her to the door and we both get into her car. When we make it across town to where our nail salon is, I frown when she pulls into a parking lot across the street. When I see the name of the business she pulls in front of, I shake my head. "You think *I'm* hardheaded? You're relentless."

"Whatever. You'll thank me later."

"It's Saturday, Brie. I'm not waiting around here all day," I tell her as she opens the door.

"Don't worry about that. I sent Mandy, who always takes care of me, a text. She knows you're coming," she says cheerfully, and I groan.

"I hate you." I shift awkwardly after taking a seat in the dark theater.

"Oh, stop. It's not that bad." Brie laughs, grabbing the menu and glancing over it.

"Not that bad? Are you insane? I feel like my whole…." I look around, then hiss, "She didn't even ask what I wanted. She just took it all."

"Give it a few hours. The uncomfortableness will go away. When that happens, you're going to be singing 'A Whole New World' at the top of your lungs."

"Whatever." I shift again then press the button on the side of my chair. When the waiter arrives, I ask him to bring me two glasses of wine and an order of nachos with extra jalapenos, and Brie asks for a Diet Coke and a popcorn with extra butter.

"I can't wait for tomorrow," Brie says when the waiter leaves, and I glance over at her.

"Why? What's going on?"

"Um, hello? Cobi is coming to your house tonight and you just got a wax job."

"I'm not having sex with him, Brie."

"Sure you're not." She smirks at me.

"I'm not," I state firmly as my stomach twists. I can't even fathom the idea of sleeping with Cobi. If one brush from his lips sent me into a tailspin, sex with him would likely leave me brainless.

"Yet," Brie mumbles, but I ignore her and focus all my attention on the movie as it begins to play.

When the movie comes to an end, I look over at Brie and we both grin. "Chris Pratt is so hot."

"So hot," I agree with a cheesy smile.

"Cobi is hotter."

"Here we go again."

"Just sayin'." She grabs her purse, and I grab mine off the chair next to me. "Cobi could totally give Chris a run for his money."

"Does Kenyon know that you've become obsessed with Cobi?"

"My man knows exactly what he gives me. Trust me, he is not concerned." She smiles at me over her shoulder as we walk down the stairs.

"Good to know." I laugh as we head out the front doors of the theater. Halfway across the parking lot, the hairs on the back of my neck stand on end and I look around for the source of my unease. I shake off the feeling and open the door when I don't notice anyone or anything that would make me uncomfortable.

"You okay?" Brie asks as I buckle my seat belt.

"Yeah, just a weird feeling." A shiver slides down my spine.

"Weird feeling?"

"I think it's just the parking lot and what happened. Ya know?"

"I didn't even think. I should have remembered," she says, looking worried.

"It's okay. I'm okay." I rest my hand over hers. "Trust me, I'm fine. It's just going to take time."

"I'm going to call Monday and set up your appointment."

"Okay."

"Okay?" she asks, surprised by my easy agreement.

"I know I need to talk about it. I'm not looking forward to it, but I know I need to talk about what happened."

"I'm here for you. Whatever you need, I'm here for you and so is Ken."

"I know," I agree with a shaky breath.

"Let's get you home." She puts the key in the ignition then starts up her car. When we pull out of the parking space, I swear I feel eyes on me and look around but don't see anyone. I try to push the feeling aside, but until I get home and into my house, that feeling only seems to grow more intense.

Cobi

Chapter 5

WITH A PIZZA BOX tucked between my bicep and hand, and a case of beer in my grasp, I make my way up toward Hadley's front door. When I see that all the lights in her place are once again on, my jaw tightens. I hate that she's living in fear. I hate that she's afraid to even be in her own home alone. I hate it worse that there is nothing I can really do but be here for her until she talks everything out and finds a way to move past what she went through. Knowing I can't protect her from her own mind makes me feel helpless, a feeling I've never felt before.

Then again, she seems to bring a lot of feelings out of me that I have never felt in the past. Protective, possessive, and a little crazy with lust. When I'm not with her, I'm thinking about her, and when I'm with her, I'm thinking about all the things I want to be doing to her. Not only is she sweet, but she's the sexiest woman I have ever met, with brains and a smart mouth that seems to leave me panting after her like a lost dog.

When I reach her front door, I ring the bell and wait while looking through the glass at the side. I watch her approach, and my cock twitches behind my zipper. Normally when I come over, she's already dressed for bed, but tonight she's dressed, wearing tight jeans that are destroyed from ankle to thigh, showing skin sporadically, with a tight tank top that leaves little to the imagination. As her eyes meet mine through the glass, I watch a million emotions filter through her gaze—lust, confusion, and apprehension, the strongest of the three.

"Hey," I greet. Before she can open her mouth to reply, I dip my head and brush my lips against hers. Fuck, her lips are soft, so fucking soft I want to spend weeks or maybe years exploring their texture. Even though I want to, I don't stop to study the look on her face after I've kissed her. Instead, I head for her kitchen, which is open to her small living room, and drop the pizza on the counter. When I turn, I find that she's still standing at the door with it wide open, her eyes on me, looking dazed.

"Honey, you might wanna close that." Jumping suddenly, she slams the door closed quickly and shakes her head like she's trying to right her thoughts, and I fight back a smile. "Got us a half extra cheese, half everything, 'cause I didn't know what you liked," I tell her as she starts toward me.

"I like it all," she says. "Though, extra cheese is always a win in my book."

"Good to know." I watch her as she gets closer to me and can tell she's nervous—something she hasn't been the two times I've been here before. "How was today?"

She lets out a breath then shakes her head. "Good, if you don't count Brie bringing you up nonstop."

"She likes me," I state with a shrug.

"Yeah," she agrees, looking annoyed. My smile turns into a grin and she drops her eyes to my mouth briefly. "Then again, she hasn't been around you when you're annoying. My guess, when that happens, her feelings toward you will change."

"We'll see," I mutter, opening the lid on the box on the counter. "Hungry?"

"I wasn't, but now I am," she says, eyeing the pizza before she grabs plates from one of the cupboards. I open a beer for myself and offer her one, but she shakes her head. I place four slices of pizza on my plate then watch her place three on hers before grabbing a bottle of water and heading toward the couch. I follow her and take a seat as she picks up the remote and turns on the TV.

"How was your day?"

At her quietly spoken question, I turn my head to look at her and fight the urge to drag her closer and kiss her again. "My mom's getting ready for a big yard sale and wanted to go through things in one of the storage lockers she owns. Dad knew she'd have him dragging everything out, so he asked me to help." At her confused look, I fill in the blanks. "My mom owns a store in town and she never throws anything away, even things that should be tossed, she holds on to them. She's been saying for years she's going to have a yard sale."

"Better late than never." She laughs, and hearing her beautiful laughter for the first time, I know I want to hear it every day for the rest of my life.

"It's been ten years, baby."

"Well then, I want to know when she plans on having it. Maybe she will be selling collectables."

I grin at that then shove another bite of pizza into my mouth. "Anyway, I like spending time with my old man, so it was good to do that."

"Is it just you and your parents, or do you have any siblings?"

At her question, I finish another bite from one of my slices, swallowing before answering. "One sister, her name is Hannah. She's a flight attendant. She lives in France, and most of her flights are international. She comes home a few times a year."

"Wow, so she speaks French?"

"No, not well anyway." I chuckle. "And she failed French in high school and got by on the edge of her teeth in college."

"That must be interesting for her."

"It is, but she loves it, and having been to visit her a few times over the years, I get why she's insisted on staying there."

"You've been to France?" Her voice fills with awe and her eyes light up.

"To Paris." I take a pull from my beer. "I've never traveled outside of the city when I've gone. Then again, with so much history in the city, it would take years to experience it all, so I haven't felt gypped."

"It's on my bucket list." She smiles, leaning closer, her eyes filling with excitement. "One day, I want to stand under the Eiffel Tower and watch it light up. Then I want to sit under it and eat a crêpe or twelve from one of the local vendors I've researched."

"I've had the crêpes myself and can tell you from firsthand experience the Nutella ones are the best. Then again, the lemon and sugar ones are nothing to sneeze at."

"I can't wait to experience them for myself," she mumbles before taking a bite from one of her slices.

"What about you? Do you have any siblings?"

At my question, I watch her frame freeze and her muscles tighten. "Nope, it's just me."

"What about your parents?"

Her eyes meet mine and something that looks like apprehension fills them. "My parents...." She presses her lips together then looks away briefly. "I don't see them much. They... um... they are kind of busy doing their own thing."

Reading the look on her face, I let it go and don't question what she means. I know her parents were not in her hospital room the night she was there and that they haven't been around since she's been home, at least not when I've been around. Judging by the way her body has tensed at my question, I know whatever happened between her and her parents isn't good. I also know I need to tread lightly where they're concerned.

"You've never told me what you do." I change the subject, and her body relaxes.

"I'm a social worker. I work for Giving Hearts. I've been there for the last five years."

"That's not an easy job." It's an understatement. Being a cop, I understand better than most how dedicated social workers need to be, how much time they spend protecting kids and working to bring families back together. A lot of love goes into the job, and they don't always get the credit they deserve for the time and energy they put into their work.

"No it's not, but I love what I do. It's rewarding in its own ways, and knowing I'm helping kids is what really matters to me."

"What you do is important."

"Yeah," she agrees with a slight shrug, like she's not comfortable with my praise, and then her eyes go to the TV. "Nothing is on. Are you okay with watching the Hallmark Channel?"

"Do I get a choice?" My response is sarcastic, and her giggle is instant.

"You don't like the Hallmark Channel?" She turns to look at me.

"Lovey-dovey shows aren't really my thing," I mutter, listening to her laugh again.

"It's a mystery." I look at her once more when I feel her eyes on me. "I think even you might like it."

Fuck, I like her. She's a mystery to me. A mystery I want to spend the rest of my life trying to solve. I have never met another woman like her. I've never met a woman who leaves me questioning everything. A woman who leaves me wanting more of whatever she's willing to give me.

"We'll see," I mumble, and she smiles before looking away. I focus—or try to focus—on the show, but with her so close, just out of arm's reach, it's hard to do. After I've eaten the pizza off my plate and finished my beer, I set my plate on her coffee table and lean back. When she sets her plate down, I don't think; I hook her around her shoulders and pull her into my side without asking her for permission. She tenses, but after a few minutes, her body relaxes, her head comes to rest against my chest, and her hand slides over my stomach.

I watch the television, not really seeing it at all. My mind and body are hyperaware of every inch of her pressed against me. I never thought I'd be sitting with a woman like this, thinking the things I'm thinking. I know it's too soon, but I also know without a doubt that I could spend every evening for the rest of my life with her curled against me, with her scent of peaches bringing me peace, with us doing nothing but just this.

When the movie comes to an end, she tips her head back toward me. I study her small smile, gorgeous face, and beautiful eyes, and then without thinking, I touch my lips to hers. I hear her sharp intake of breath and feel her fingers wrap tightly around my side. I don't move away; I swipe my tongue across the seam of her lips then groan in approval when her tongue comes out to touch my own.

"Cobi," she breathes my name against my mouth, making my cock jerk in response.

Fuck. I have never heard anything hotter than my name on her lips. Without thought, I move my hand into her hair to hold her in place then I kiss her again, deeper than before, thrusting my tongue between her lips. She doesn't hesitate. She doesn't pull away. She kisses me back. Her fingers curl into my tee and her nails dig into my skin, making me rock-hard. I move her, lifting her up to straddle my lap, and nip her bottom lip when she rolls her hips against mine. My cock jerks, and my hands on her hips tighten.

I should probably stop this. I know I should at the very least slow this down, but with every whimper, every moan, every flick of her tongue against mine, I'm fighting a losing battle. Since the moment she looked into my eyes, I knew who she was to me, knew exactly what she meant for my future. Knew she was *mine*.

Sliding my hand around her hip, I slip it down between her jeans and stomach then watch her back arch, and growl, "You're so fucking soft everywhere." When my fingers find her clit, my cock jumps against my zipper.

I roll my fingers and listen to her moan. "Please don't stop," she begs as her hips jerk, and I bite back a curse. She's silky smooth and wet, so fucking wet that I can smell it, so fucking wet that I know if I got my face between her legs, my mouth would fill with her juices and her taste would be with me for days. "God, don't stop." Her nails dig into my skin.

"Ride it out, beautiful. Show me what you look like when you come," I urge, using my hand on her hip to rock her hard against my fingers.

Her lips part, and her eyes open to half-mast and meet mine, the heat in them searing me to my core. Fuck, she's the most beautiful thing I've ever seen in my life. "I…."

"Don't fucking stop." I rock her harder against me as I slip one finger then another into her hot, tight, wet heat. "Fuck, you're so damn hot, so damn wet. I can't wait to taste this." I roll my thumb over her clit, causing her hips to buck and a whimper to escape her lips. "Can't fucking wait to feel this cunt squeezing my cock. Do you know how untfl COBI

good it's going to feel when I slide inside you? Know how good it's going to feel when I fill you full with me?" Her pussy spasms around my fingers at my words, and I tighten my hold on her. "Jesus, baby, this pussy was made for me."

She clutches my shoulders tighter and rides my hand, moaning my name.

"Christ, baby, you're going to make me come in my jeans just from watching you." Her eyes flare and her mouth opens, but before she can speak, I lean forward and bite her nipple through her tank, causing her to gasp.

"Oh, God." Her head falls back to her shoulders as her pussy tightens around my fingers.

"Look at me, Hadley." Her head drops forward and her eyes meet mine. "Christ, I want to have you naked over me in this exact position. I want to watch your tits bouncing in my face, your hair wild and flowing over your shoulders. I want your legs spread so that I can watch you take me. Then I want to watch myself disappear into your pussy over and over until your juices are coating my cock." I lean forward until my mouth is almost against hers. "Then I want to watch as you find your release using me, before I use your body to find my own."

"Cobi!" she cries out with her hips moving in sync with my fingers.

"Give me your mouth then give me your orgasm, Hadley." Her pupils dilate, her lips part slightly, and her chest heaves. When she doesn't give me what I want, I stop thrusting my fingers and rolling her clit. "Give me what I want." Her eyes darken then her mouth drops down to mine as she slides her soft hand around the back of my neck then up into my hair, touching her tongue to mine.

I force her to ride my fingers hard as I kiss her, thrusting my tongue back into her mouth. When her pussy starts to spasm, I pull my mouth from hers so I can watch her expression as she comes.

"Yes." She gasps for breath, looking into my eyes before she drops her forehead to mine. When her breathing evens out, I slowly pull my fingers from her then wrap my arms around her waist and hold her against my chest, running my hand up and down her back. I expect her to freak, to tell me that what happened was a mistake and I need to leave, but soon I realize she's fallen asleep. I close my eyes for a moment then carefully stand with her in my arms and head toward her bedroom. I lay her down in her bed, and she doesn't even twitch as I pull her blanket over her and turn on her sound machine, casting the room with a blue glow. I leave her in her bedroom, shutting the door and ignoring my still hard cock and the urge to get into bed with her. Over the years, my gut has never led me wrong, and right now, it's telling me I'm moving too quickly and that if I move any faster or push her any harder, she will run and I will have to spend a whole lot of fucking time trying to catch her again.

When I'm cleaning up the kitchen and our plates, my cell phone beeps in my pocket. I pull it out and read the text, scrubbing one hand through my hair in frustration. Frank and I have been investigating a string of break-ins across town for the last couple of weeks, and tonight a suspect was apprehended by a homeowner who was not okay with a man breaking into his house. After I call Frank to let him know I'm on my way, I shove my phone back into my pocket. I debate just leaving Hadley a note to let her know I'm gone, but worry she will wake up and freak when I'm not here like I have been the last two nights. I open the door to her bedroom and walk to the bed, taking a seat in the crook of her lap and pushing the hair away from her face. When her eyes flutter open, I lean in close to her.

"I gotta go, baby."

"You're leaving?" She sits up suddenly, almost plowing into me in her haste to turn on the lamp. When her worried eyes meet mine, my stomach knots. "Is… is everything okay?"

"I've been working a case for a few weeks, and tonight a suspect was apprehended. I need to go in and interview him."

"Oh." She swallows then nods. "Okay."

"You want me to come back when I'm done?"

Her body freezes along with her breath. I can tell she doesn't want to admit she wants that, but I know instinctively that she wants me here with her. "You don't have to do that. I'll be okay."

"I'll be back." I force her back an inch as I lean in closer. "I'll take a key. That way, if you're sleeping, I can just let myself in."

"You...." She shakes her head and takes a shuddered breath. "Really, that isn't necessary." Her beautiful eyes meet mine, but I don't miss as she grips the bedding between her fingers. "I appreciate it, but I'm sure you have a home and a bed of your own you probably miss. I'll be okay tonight if you go home after you're done."

"I'm coming back." I don't tell her I have an empty house and an even lonelier bed, that even Maxim—my hundred pound bullmastiff—isn't home, because he's been staying with my parents, since I have been working so much and don't like leaving him alone for long. "I don't know how late I will be, but I'll be back at some point tonight."

"Cobi—" She licks her lips.

"Where do you have a key?" I cut her off before she can attempt to sway me again.

She studies me for a long moment then lets out a deep breath. "I have a spare key in the drawer next to the fridge. It has a Disney key ring attached to it."

"Right." I smile, and her gaze drops to my mouth briefly.

"Um... will you come in here and let me know when you get back, so I don't freak out if I hear you out there in the living room walking around?"

"I can do that." I stand then lean over her, planting a fist in the bed on each side of her hips. "Try to get some sleep. I'll leave all the lights on in the living room, so you don't have to worry."

"Thanks, Cobi."

"No problem, baby. Rest. I'll see you soon." I kiss her forehead then tip her head back with my knuckles under her chin and touch my mouth to hers before leaving her room, then shutting the door without another look at her in her bed.

I grab her spare key from the drawer next to the fridge then keep all the lights on like I said I would before I leave, locking the door. I scan the street and feel some of the tension leave when I don't see the media parked anywhere on her block. I haven't heard Hadley's name mentioned the last few times I've caught the news. The story of what happened to Harmony has turned mostly toward what happened at the hospital with Dr. Hofstadter, something I'm thankful for, since I'm not sure how Hadley would deal if the press was hounding her like they've done to my cousin. Where Harmony has her fiancé and our family to protect her, Hadley as far as I can see has no one but her best friend and now me.

I rub my hand over my chest at that realization, then hit the unlock button for my truck. When I get in behind the wheel, I stare at Hadley's house for a long moment before starting the engine. As I back out of her driveway, I have to remind myself I'm leaving her alone for just for a little while, not forever.

Hadley ━━ Cobi

Chapter 6

FEAR GRIPS MY CHEST as I listen to Cobi leave and the front door close. I sit in the middle of my bed, with my heart beating wildly, and I fight the urge to get up and run after him, to beg him to stay or to take me with him. I have never been weak. I have never needed someone to tell me everything will be okay, until now. I close my eyes and silently remind myself there is no one after me, that I'm safe at home in my bed, behind solid walls, a locked door, and closed windows. When my eyes open, I feel a little better and start to lie back, but I realize I'm still dressed.

That's when it happens. That's when I remember what Cobi and I did on my couch. That's when I remember the most spectacular orgasm of my life brought on by him, his fingers, and his dirty words.

Obviously with the fear that took over on the thought of him leaving, I didn't think about what we did or what I wanted to do before I apparently fell asleep and he tucked me in. My eyes close and heat creeps up my cheeks. I thought before that it was difficult being around him, but now I have no idea how the hell I will ever face him again.

"With the way you acted, he probably thinks you're a floozy, that you do that kind of thing all the time—just let random men touch you and bring you to orgasm." I groan, lying back and pulling my pillow over my face. No man has ever given me what he did; no man has ever turned me on to the point I lost rational thought. No man has brought me to orgasm with a few words and a couple of strokes from their fingers. Then again, none of the men I have been with even came close to being a guy like Cobi. A man who vocalizes what he wants, what he needs, and demands compliance with a simple look. Just thinking about the things he said and did to me makes my body tingle and core tighten. "This is not good, Hadley, so totally not good," I say while pulling my pillow from my face.

Still feeling the aftermath of my orgasm between my legs, I get up and take a quick shower then change into one of my nightgowns. Knowing Cobi will be back, I put on my robe, tying it tightly around my waist before I get back into bed. I lie there forever, waiting to hear him return. I try to think of what I will say to him when I see him, but before I can come up with some kind of explanation for my sudden sluttiness, I fall asleep.

My feet feel like they're sinking into concrete as I try to run.

I open my mouth to scream, but no sound escapes.

I fight for breath, listening to the falls of his feet on the forest floor bringing him closer to my hiding spot.

"I can hear you breathing."

I hold my breath when his voice echoes through the darkness surrounding me.

"I'll find you, bitch. I will fucking find you and end you."

An ear-shattering gunshot goes off, echoing through the quiet, and debris from one of the trees surrounding me scrapes against my skin, burning into my flesh.

I gasp for air as I sit up, holding my hand against my chest.

I fumble for the light next to the bed, knocking my lamp over in my haste and hear the delicate glass shatter against the floor as my lungs beg for oxygen. I toss the blankets away from my overheated body then throw my legs over the side of the bed and stand. I don't acknowledge the shards of glass cutting into my bare feet as I stumble to the bathroom. I flip on the light and turn on the cold water, cupping my hands and tossing it toward my face, wanting to wash away the memories of my dream. When my breathing has evened out and I've rid myself of my nightmare, I fall to my knees then lie down and curl into a ball on the floor in my bathroom. As a shiver slides down my spine and cold seeps into my skin from the floor, I pull one of my towels over me like a blanket and hug it to my chest.

"Hadley?" My name is called as tears skim down my cheeks, and I stare at the white tiled shower wall across the room, unblinking. "Hadley?" The bathroom door presses against my back. Then, before I even take my next breath, I'm up off the ground and cocooned in strong arms and settled against Cobi's hard chest. "Fuck, I'm so fucking sorry," he whispers against the side of my head, and I close my eyes tightly, feeling safety and warmth slide through every cell in my body. When he settles into my bed with his back against my headboard, my eyes open. I see the room around us cast in blue and hear the soft sound of the ocean coming from my sound machine, making this feel like a dream.

"He was chasing me," I whisper, tipping my head back to look into a set of worried eyes. "I couldn't get away or scream." My eyes slide closed and I bury my face against his chest. "I heard his gun go off and felt it, felt the bark from the trees around me cutting into my skin."

"You're safe now, Hadley."

"I know," I agree, burrowing deeper into him. "I...." I pull in a shuddering breath. "It felt so real, like I was back there."

His warm hand roams down my back, and his softly spoken words seep into my skin. "You're not there. You're here with me, safe in my arms, right where you're supposed to be. You're safe, Hadley."

Fresh tears fill my eyes and my grip on him tightens. He's right, but he's also completely wrong, because as safe as I feel in his arms, I also feel more afraid than I have in my entire life. I pull in a shaky breath, not sure what I'm going to say, but knowing I need to say something to him. But before I can open my mouth, his body goes rigid and his grip on me tightens almost painfully.

"What is it?" I ask.

"You're bleeding. Where are you bleeding?"

"What?" I blink as he jostles me in his arms then listen to him curse when he notices the lamp is not on the table but on the floor next to the bed.

"Did you cut your feet?" I don't have a chance to answer him before he carefully sets me away and gets up. Then I watch him stalk to the light switch and flip it on. His gaze zeros in on my feet, and I cringe at the sight of blood that has dotted my sheets and blankets. "Shit," he growls, coming back toward me and scooping me up out of bed like I weigh nothing at all. Going to the bathroom, he flips on the light then sets me down on the edge of the vanity. "Do you have a first aid kit?"

"No, but I have some Band-Aids in one of these drawers." I start to hop down to find them, but he stops me, wrapping his hands around my waist.

My breath stutters as he places his face an inch from mine. "Stay put. I have a kit in my truck. I'll be right back."

"I…" I lick my lips, trying to fight the urge to lean in and place my mouth to his. "I think I just need to wash my feet off. The cuts don't look that bad."

"Stay put," he orders, kisses my forehead, and then disappears.

"Stay put? What the hell am I, a dog?"

"I heard that," I hear him say, and I roll my eyes toward the ceiling. Not even two minutes later, he comes back in carrying a large plastic case that he sets on the vanity and opens. I watch him pull out a bottle of alcohol and a roll of gauze then turn on the tap. My eyes widen when he wraps his arm under my knees and lifts my legs so that my feet are in the sink. I bite the inside of my cheek when the water hits the open cuts.

"This might burn a little." He turns off the water then pours the alcohol on my open wounds, making me jump and cry out.

"A little?" I shout. "It feels like my feet are on fire now." I grip his forearm and dig my nails into his skin. "Oh my God, blow on it or something, you jerk!" I continue to yell, and he laughs. "This isn't funny."

"Breathe, the burn will ease in a second."

"Says the guy who's not being tortured," I grouch, watching him smile. "I hate you." I place my arms behind me when he lifts one foot then the other. When he touches one of the cuts, I flinch.

"The cuts aren't deep, but this one has a piece of glass in it that I need to get out."

"Great, more torture. Are you enjoying this?"

His eyes meet mine, and the look in them is so intense my breathing stops. "I'd never enjoy hurting you."

My quiet "Okay" is barely audible as we stare at each other. With a jerk of his chin, he pulls his eyes from mine then digs out a pair of tweezers from his kit. I watch the muscle in his cheek jump as he carefully and painlessly pulls the piece of splintered glass from my foot, and then groan when he lifts the bottle of alcohol. "Is that really necessary? You already did it once."

"Sorry, baby, I'm not taking any chances." Without warning, he pours the cold liquid over my skin and I flinch from the burn. When he's done, and the burning has eased, he dries off both my feet. I sigh in relief when he tears open a few packets of ointment and slathers my skin before starting to wrap my feet with gauze.

"Thank goodness I don't have to work tomorrow. If I did, I would look like an idiot wearing heels having mummy feet," I tell him, and he looks at me briefly and smiles. At his smile, my heart does a double beat inside my chest and my body gets warm from head to toe. I know if I turned and looked at myself in the mirror I'd look like a bright red tomato. "Um… I think I need to say something about what happened earlier," I start, needing to fill the silence in the bathroom.

"You don't unless you want to," he states, setting down one foot when he's done wrapping it and picking up the other.

"I don't really want to talk about it, but I want you to know that… I… umm." Crap, how do I tell him that I'm not a hussy?

"You don't have to say anything, Hadley. I know that what you're going through is difficult, and that until you talk to someone it's going to keep messing with your head. It will get easier."

"Oh." I bite my lip, wondering if I should just let it go, let him think that's what I wanted to talk about. No, I can't. I don't think I will be able to be around him if he thinks less of me, especially when I seem to need him as much as I do. "It's not that."

"Excuse me?" He looks at me once more, his hands on my foot

pausing mid-wrap.

"It's about what happened on the couch. I…. Well, I just want you to know I don't normally…" My cheeks burn even hotter as his eyes roam my face. "Well, I don't do that kind of thing, like ever." I squeeze my eyes closed then open them back up. "I mean, obviously I do that kind of thing. I mean, I don't… but I have done it." My eyes narrow on his. "Why are you smiling?"

"A few different reasons. But please continue."

"I don't think I want to now."

"I can wait." He shrugs, going back to my foot.

I stare at him for a long time, expecting him to ask me what I was going to say. When I realize he's not going to, I give in. "Fine." I let out a huff. "I just wanted to say I'm not normally that slutty." His hands pause again and his head turns toward me. When his eyes meet mine and the words I just spoke register in my own head, I know I'm officially past embarrassment. "I'm just going to shut up now."

"You're not slutty, and I would never think you are. What happened between us was good, so don't try to twist it in your head into something bad, 'cause that will piss me off," he growls, his eyes blazing with something I have never seen before. "We've got chemistry. It was bound to happen. Was it too soon? Maybe. Will it happen again? Fuck yes, it will."

"I…" Holy cow. Why the heck did I open my mouth? "I don't know if that's smart, Cobi."

"You don't have to know, because I do."

"You seem… umm… pretty sure."

"Never been more sure of anything in my life." He pulls his eyes from mine then finishes wrapping my foot, having no idea the effect his words have had on me. When he's done, he leaves the mess on the counter and picks me up, carrying me to my bed. Stopping at the side of it, he holds me in his arms then grumbles something I can't make out before carrying me to the living room and placing me on the couch. "Stay here, I'm going to clean up the glass. You got an extra set of sheets somewhere?"

Stunned, I nod then point him in the direction of the hall closet where

I keep my towels and extra bedding. I listen to him moving around, and then hear the sound of my vacuum start up. I watch the clock on the wall as I wait for him to finish, wanting to get up and help but having no doubt if I tried he'd carry me right back in here. When he's finished, he comes back to get me then carries me to bed, setting me down. I'm surprised at the way he made the bed; most men I know of wouldn't bother tucking in the top sheet or folding down the edge of the blanket.

"Thank you, again."

"It's not a big deal." He shrugs as he takes off his badge, dropping it to my bedside table then doing the same with his cell phone.

I glance at both items then look up as he's unclasping his belt and sliding it from his jeans. "Are you staying in here?"

"Yep." Well, okay. Now what the hell do I do? I should play the non-hussy and tell him to sleep on the couch, but offer him a pillow and blanket, since he's been so nice. I should probably do that, but I don't. I don't, because the reality is I want him close. I feel better when he's around, safer even from my own mind when he's near me.

"Okay." I scoot over to the middle of the bed, and he smiles a soft smile before rolling over to turn out the light.

When he comes back, he lies down then tugs me into his side, leaving me no choice but to curl into him. Then he picks up his phone and I watch him set an alarm.

"That's just four hours from now," I inform him as he clicks off his phone and drops it back to the side table.

"Yeah, but I gotta get to work in the morning. Before that, I need to head to my place to shower and change."

"I'm really messing with your life."

"Yeah you are," he agrees, and guilt hits me hard and fast. I know he has his parents; I know he has a cousin, aunt, and uncle. I also know he has a place of his own. Still, he's spent the last three nights with me, taking care of me and bringing me dinner. "Don't twist that, Hadley." His arm tightens around my shoulders. "I wouldn't have it any other way. There is nowhere else I want to be."

My chest feels funny, as I wheeze out, "You kind of freak me out."

"I know." He lets out a breath. "You'll get used to it."

"Will I?"

"Yeah, eventually." I hear a smile in his voice, and I want to look at him to see his expression, but I don't. "Sleep."

"You know, you're also kind of bossy."

"Figure you'll get used to that too."

I don't snort or roll my eyes, even though I want to. I definitely don't tell him that I won't get used to it because this won't work between us. As good as this feels, I need to fight it. I need to remember where I come from, who I come from. I know that if Cobi ever finds out about my family, his opinion of me will change, and he will look at me like every other man I've told about my past has—with contempt and horror.

"You're safe, Hadley." He reads the tightening in my body, thinking I'm scared, and my eyes squeeze closed. Seriously, he's sweet.

When his lips brush the top of my head, I burrow closer to him without a word, telling myself that tomorrow I'll pull away and put up my walls against him. But tonight, I'm going to sleep in his arms and pretend this could work out, like if he found out about my past he wouldn't care.

Chapter 7

WHEN MY CELL PHONE buzzes in my purse, I continue to work and ignore it like I've done all day today, feeling nauseous when the buzzing stops then starts up again. Yesterday morning, Cobi left early, giving me a sweet kiss to my forehead then lips before telling me that he would see me later. After he was gone, I laid in bed for a long time in a sleepy, happy daze, still feeling the lingering of his soft kiss to my lips.

It wasn't until I got up, had a cup of coffee, and in my happy haze answered my phone that reality came crashing down around me. Normally, I never answer when I see one of my parents is calling, but I answered without thinking and immediately wished I hadn't. At just ten in the morning, my dad was drunk and probably high. He slurred as he asked me if I had really been shot at by—in his words—some fucked up doctor.

After my answer of yes and explaining to him what happened, he asked if he could borrow some money to help pay his and Mom's electric bill that is overdue. His non-reaction wasn't a surprise; still, it hurt that he didn't really care if I was okay or that I could've died.

I'm sure the only reason he called was to ask for money. Finding out if the rumors were true was just a bonus. After I told him no, that I didn't have money to help him with the electric bill, he hung up on me, but not before I listened to him mutter about how ungrateful I've always been. It wasn't a surprise that my mom didn't call demanding answers, since where mothers are concerned she's the worst of the worst. She should never have had kids, and thankfully after me she never had another. My dad, on the other hand, has three more kids, each with a different woman.

I didn't technically lie when I told Cobi it's just me and that I don't have siblings. I have never met my three younger brothers, and probably never will. Each of the women who had kids with my dad smartly left after realizing what a lowlife he is and that in the end he's stuck with my mom or they are stuck with each other.

My parents are still married, probably because divorce is expensive, but they are no longer in a relationship and haven't been for years. They do share the trailer I grew up in, and both live there when they are not leeching off someone they're hooking up with. My dad sells drugs from time to time, when someone is stupid enough to trust him with their product and money, and my mom works at a local bar and has since I can remember. How she's kept a job for so long when she's almost always wasted is anyone's guess, but she's done it.

My desk phone ringing pulls me from my thoughts, and I reach out, grab it, and put it to my ear. "Hadley speaking."

"Ugh, I just thought I'd warn you," Brie starts, sounding worried, and I sit up in my chair as she continues. "I was leaving the parking lot and saw what looks like a very pissed off Cobi Mayson heading into the office."

"What?" I look around for someplace to hide, and then my eyes widen when I spot Cobi talking to one of my co-workers whose desk is near the front door and see him flash his badge.

"I think you left a whole lot of stuff out last night," Brie says in my ear, and I pull in a shaky breath.

"I'll explain later. Right now, I need to find a place to hide."

"Good luck with that. With how pissed off that man looks, the moon wouldn't be far enough away for you to escape him." She hangs up and I drop the phone into the cradle as Cobi turns to look at me.

When his dark, angry eyes meet mine, I know not only is he pissed—I'm screwed.

Last night, I put my plan to keep Cobi away into action. I didn't stay at home; instead, I took Brie up on her offer and slept at Kenyon's and her place. Luckily, I didn't have to sleep on the couch, since she bought an air mattress just for me in case I came over. When she asked about Cobi, I said he was working then avoided all conversation having to do with him, changing the subject each and every time. If I ever told her my plan to keep him at arm's length and gave her my reasons for doing it, she would be mad. Actually, she would be livid. Even as long as she's been in my life, she's never really understood why I'm so ashamed. She thinks I should be proud of who I am, how far I've come, and look at the bright side of things.

She doesn't know how humiliating it is to have to explain my past. She doesn't know how embarrassing it is to have one or both my parents show up unannounced and make a scene. Something they have done more than once when I haven't given them what they wanted. No guy wants to deal with that. No guy wants a woman who has the kind of baggage I have. And a cop would for sure not be happy about having a girlfriend with druggie, alcoholic parents that have been arrested so many times most officers and judges know them by name.

Not seeing a place to escape, I stand and watch Cobi stalk toward my office, his long stride eating up the distance between us quickly. Crap, things would be a whole lot easier if he wasn't so damn attractive. Even angry, he's hot, maybe even hotter, with his jaw hard and his muscles seeming more pronounced. When he steps through my open door, I start to open my mouth, having no idea what I will say to him, but I shut it as he slams the door closed, causing the pictures on the walls to shake.

"What the fuck?" His voice booms through my small office, and I look over his shoulder, noticing my co-workers stopping to take in the scene.

"Keep your voice down," I hiss, swinging my head back to look at him. "This is my job. You can't just barge in here, slam doors, and shout at me."

"Where were you last night?" he demands, and I pull in a breath, wanting to calm my wildly beating heart. "Answer me."

"I stayed with Brie. She wanted me to stay with her and Kenyon. They've been worried about me."

"Lie."

How the hell does he know I'm lying?

"It's not a lie."

"Part of it's not, and part of it is." He crosses his arms over his chest. "Now tell me why you're avoiding me?"

"I'm not avoiding you." I scoff, and his eyes narrow.

"Another lie."

"You don't know me, Cobi," I hiss, getting angry and defensive.

"How many lies are you going to tell me before you start telling the truth?"

"That is not a lie. You don't know me. We don't even really know each other."

"I know what you sound and look like when you come."

Oh my God. He did not just say that. "Don't be crass." I hiss, pointing at him.

Ignoring me, he continues, still holding my gaze. "Know you try to be brave but are so fucking afraid that you're scared of the dark. Know that you turn sweet when you're sleepy and don't know how to handle being taken care of. I also know that you like me more than you want to, and that scares the shit out of you."

"I don't like you," I whisper, his words hitting too close to home, making me feel panicked.

"Another fucking lie." He shakes his head. "Why are you so afraid of me?" He leans closer, growling, "Why?"

"I can't do this right now," I state, leaving out that I will never be able to do this. "I'm at work. I have to leave to go check on a client soon, and before that, I have a hundred e-mails to return."

Jerking a hand through his hair, he looks away briefly. "Hadley, you need to know that even if I let you go right now, I'm not letting you go. We will be having this conversation, and you will talk to me."

I ignore the way my stomach clenches and shake my head. "We'll talk."

"When?"

Never.

"Later, just not right now, not when I'm at work and not with all my co-workers watching," I say, not even having to look out my office window to see that all eyes are still on us.

"Another lie." He looks away pushing his fingers through his hair. "I'll be at your place tonight, at eight. Gonna warn you baby if you're not there and I have to track you down, I'm going to be pissed."

"You're already pissed," I point out the obvious, then fight the urge to take a step back when his jaw twitches and his eyes darken.

"I spent all night worried about you, worried if you were sleeping, worried if you had another nightmare, worried that no one would be there for you if you did. All fucking night, I tossed and turned, unable to sleep because of you. So yeah, I'm fucking pissed."

He spent the whole night worried about me? Why does that make my stomach feel warm? Without me even trying, the tension leaves my muscles and my body softens. "I'm sorry," I say quietly. "I should have called you to tell you I was okay."

"Did you sleep?"

I look away then bite my lip before I shake my head. I tried to sleep, but I couldn't. I was so afraid of having a nightmare that I laid awake all night, pretending to watch TV while thinking about him. I really hate that he did the same thing.

"When is your first doctor's appointment?"

"What?" I look at him, confused by his change of subject.

"Your appointment, the one Brie is setting up for you. When is it?"

Crap, of course he remembers that I told him I was going to talk to someone. "Today, after I get off work."

"Good, baby," he says softly as his expression gentles.

God, I love when his voice goes soft like that, really love the look on his face right now. I don't say that. Instead, I whisper, "I really need to work, Cobi, but I hope you know I'm truly sorry for making you worry last night. I should have thought about that and at least called to tell you I was okay."

"I'll call us even if you stop avoiding me now." I don't agree out loud, since that would be a lie and he might confront me again. Instead, I nod once. "Even not speaking out loud, you're a shit liar."

Seriously, how the hell does he know when I'm lying? I don't have a tick or a tell; I don't twirl my hair or get a twitch under my eye. "Are we done?"

"Not by a long shot." He uncrosses his arms. "Still, I'll let you get back to work."

"Thanks." I fight the need to roll my eyes at him.

"See you tonight."

"Yep." I nod.

He shakes his head and his lips twitch. I don't know what he finds funny, but I can tell he is finding something entertaining. "Later, baby." He turns and leaves, opening and closing the door.

I try not to feel disappointed that he didn't even try to touch or kiss me, as I take a seat at my desk. And I avoid looking out into the main office, where I can feel eyes on me. I try to get back to work, having a hard time doing it, because I keep thinking about him. Eventually, I pull myself together enough to answer the e-mails flooding my inbox. Once I'm done in the office, I head out to check on my clients—a couple who recently adopted a newborn baby girl. I spend some time with them, making sure they're settling in okay, then leave for my doctor's appointment across town, something I'm not at all looking forward to.

Feeling drained, I leave Dr. Sprat's office at ten after six, giving his secretary a small wave before heading out to the parking lot. I had no idea what my appointment today would be like. I really had no clue that Dr. Sprat would not only get me to open up about what happened to Harmony and me, but also find a way to get me to talk about my past and my parents. The whole thing was tiring, but if I'm honest with myself, it felt good to talk to someone who isn't biased and doesn't know me. When he asked me to come back in a few days to talk some more, I didn't tell him no. Instead, I agreed to see him again.

I head for my car, digging my keys out of my purse, and then stop midstep to look around when I feel like someone is watching me. "Seriously?" I whisper, spotting Cobi leaning against my car with his arms crossed over his chest and his eyes on me through the dim light coming from the street lamps in the parking lot. "It's starting to feel like you're stalking me," I call out to him as I get a hold of my keys.

"That's probably because I am." He shrugs one shoulder like he isn't offended by my accusation.

"How did you know I was here? I know this isn't the only psychiatric practice in town."

"I called Brie. She told me where you were."

"She's seriously in so much trouble," I grumble under my breath, stopping a couple feet away from him.

"How was it?"

"How was what?"

"Your appointment."

I drag in a deep breath then let it out slowly. "Good, or whatever it's supposed to be." I lift my shoulders slightly. "I have another appointment in a few days."

"That's good." He reaches out and grabs my hand, pulling me closer to him. "I'm proud of you." I blink up at him in surprise. "It takes a lot of courage to reach out for help. Most people don't have that kind of courage."

"Thanks," I say softly while warmth floods my veins.

He reaches forward with his hand not holding mine and touches his fingers to my cheek then slides them down and across my bottom lip, making me shiver. "I hated not touching or kissing you this afternoon." At his confession, my lungs freeze. "I sat in my truck in the parking lot for a long fucking time talking myself out of going back inside again."

"You did?" My voice is breathy as I look into his eyes.

"Yeah." His finger swipes my lip once more. "Did you think about it? About not getting it from me before I left?"

I should tell him no. I should lift my hands to push him away, but instead, I nod then close my eyes as he dips his head to brush his mouth across mine.

"Softest lips I've ever felt," he murmurs. My eyes flutter open and my heart starts to pound. "I'll follow you home." He takes a slight step back, making me feel suddenly cold. "We'll order something in for dinner when we get there."

"'Kay," I agree without thinking then slide in behind the steering wheel when he opens my door. Once I'm inside, he shuts my door, and until I start the engine, he doesn't walk away. With the engine running, I watch him go to his truck parked a few spots away and get in. I pull out before him and see him in my rearview mirror, following me home.

When we reach my place, I park then get out, heading for the mailbox as he parks his truck in my driveway behind my car. After I grab the mail, I turn around and see him drag a large black duffle bag from the back. I don't ask him what's in the bag, because I already know the answer to that question. Obviously, he's planning on staying the night, but not planning on having to go home early to shower and change before work tomorrow. His assumption that he's sleeping over should annoy me, but it doesn't. Instead, I feel relieved at the idea of having him close and being able to get some sleep tonight.

When I'm halfway to my front door, my cell phone rings, so I pull it out and look at the screen. Seeing Brie's name, I know I can't ignore her call; she won't give up if I don't answer, and instead she will show up in person and demand answers. I put my phone to my ear and I pause in the middle of saying hello, watching as Cobi pulls out my spare key and opens my front door.

"Brie, I need to call you back," I say into the phone, hearing her shout "What?" before I hang up on her.

"You still have my key."

At my statement, Cobi turns to look at me over his shoulder.

His eyes roam my face and he smirks, muttering. "You didn't ask for it back."

Taking a few steps forward, I stop at the bottom of the steps, looking up at him. "I didn't know I had to ask you for my key back, since it's—" I point at myself. "—my key."

"You gave it to me."

Shaking my head, I sputter. "I didn't give it to you. I let you borrow it."

"Whatever. Do you know what you want for dinner?"

"Whatever? Seriously?" I plant my hands on my hips.

"Babe, you're exhausted. I'm exhausted and I'm also hungry. So as cute as you are when you're pissed, I don't have it in me to spar with you over a fucking key."

I ignore the whole 'you're cute' thing and focus on the rest. "I'm not sparring with you. I'm pointing out that you still have my key." I frown. "Did you use it yesterday when I wasn't home?"

"Yep," he states easily.

This guy just cannot be believed. "I want the key back," I tell him, holding out my hand and stomping up the steps to where he's standing.

"Sure." He drops it in my open palm, and I look at it then him in surprise. "Doesn't really matter; I made a copy this afternoon so you wouldn't be out a spare."

"You're crazy," I whisper. I knew him just handing me over the key was too easy. I just had no idea it was easy because he was giving me a key he already made a copy of it.

"Maybe." He shrugs before grabbing my hand and pulling me into the house. When I've cleared the door, he closes it behind me. He lets my hand go and heads toward the kitchen, leaving me staring after him.

"I think you might need some help," I tell him as he drops his duffle bag near the door to my bedroom.

When he turns to look at me, he smiles like he thinks I'm joking. "Baby."

"No, really, who does that? Who does any of the stuff you're doing?" I toss my arms up in frustration.

"A man who is interested in a woman." He shrugs then pulls out his phone. "Now, what do you want to eat? I was thinking Indian food, but really I'm good with whatever."

Looking into his eyes, I know for certain that he's not going to see how crazy he's acting, how irrational his actions are. Not having the energy to confront him and convince him that he might be insane, I go to the island he's standing near and set down my purse. "Indian sounds good."

He smiles before asking, "Do you know what you want?"

"Cheese naan, not plain, and butter chicken."

"Got it." He lifts his chin toward the cell phone still in my hand. "You might wanna call your girl back. I'm sure she's worried."

As he puts his cell phone to his ear to place our order, I shake my head and walk toward my bedroom, dialing Brie as I go. She answers on the first ring and doesn't even give me a chance to say hello before she shoots off a rapid succession of questions. I answer each one the best I can, but tell her that I will have to talk to her in person about all things Cobi, since he's only a room away. Reluctantly, she agrees after making me promise to do dinner tomorrow just her and me.

After we hang up, I change into different clothes, putting on a pair of leggings and a baggy shirt before going to the living room. Cobi is on the couch with the TV on, not watching it. Instead, his eyes are on a laptop he has resting on the coffee table in front of him. I study him for a few moments, taking in his relaxed posture and the look of concentration on his face.

He must feel me watching him, because he turns to look at me and does a head-to-toe sweep. "Everything okay with Brie?"

"Yeah, but as usual, she's worried and has questions. I promised her that I'd have dinner with her tomorrow evening."

"Are my ears going to be burning?" he asks with a small twitch of his lips.

"Probably." I shrug, and his lip twitch turns into a grin. "Do you want some water or something?" I ask, needing to do something with myself so I don't jump him.

"I'll take a beer."

"Coming right up." I go around the island to the fridge and grab him a beer then pour myself a glass of wine. When I make it back to the couch, he's shutting down his computer. "How was work?"

"Work." He shrugs, taking the beer I hold out to him. "On TV, my job seems exciting. In reality, it's a lot of paperwork and sitting behind my desk or behind the wheel of a car."

"Did you always want to be a police officer?"

"Yeah, since I can remember. What about you? Did you always want to be a social worker?"

"Yeah, in a way." I take a sip of wine before continuing. "I didn't know what a social worker was growing up, but I did always want to help kids who couldn't speak up for themselves. When I went to college, one of my counselors told me the best way to do that was to work in social services, so that's what I decided to major in." I take another sip from my wine, trying not to let the way he's looking at me affect me. "Why did you want to be a cop?"

"To protect the people I love." Those simple words and that easy statement make my chest feel like a weight has settled on it. "I thought about playing ball after high school, even had a few offers for full rides. But in the end, I knew I wouldn't be happy, so I joined the military and became an MP."

"An MP?"

"Military police officer."

I smile. "So you weren't a sharpshooter?"

"No." He smiles back. "I know the rumors. None of them are true."

"Mmm." I take a sip of wine. The rumors might not all be true, but I have no doubt there's a lot he's not saying.

When there's a knock on the door, he gets up to answer it. I expect it to be the food he ordered, but when I hear him ask, "Can I help you?" I turn to find Tom standing in the doorway.

"Hey, Tom." I get up and head around the couch. I look up at Cobi when it seems he's blocking me from the door, and explain quietly, "Tom's my landlord." Jerking up his chin, he lets me by and I shake my head.

"Got the note you left in my mailbox," Tom says shortly when I reach the door. "The answer is yes, just as long as you clean up any and all shit and pay the three hundred dollar deposit."

"Thank you," I say softly, and he grunts in response.

He turns and walks away without another word, I watch him go wondering exactly what he did for the Mob, then I smile.

"What was that about?" Cobi asks, seeing the smile on my face.

"I'm getting a dog, or maybe a cat. Either way, I'm getting an animal." I look up at him while he closes the door.

"You want a dog?"

"Well I've never owned a dog before, but I have a fenced in backyard. I owned a cat once; I miss her." His face softens. "I haven't decided what kind of animal I want. I just know I want another soul in the house so it's not so quiet when I'm home alone."

"Are you afraid of dogs?" he asks as we both go back to the couch and sit down.

"No."

"Big dogs?" he pushes.

"No, or not that I know of." My brows pull together. "Why?"

"My bullmastiff Maxim has been staying with my parents, since I've been working so much. He's housebroken and protective. You'd love him. You could keep him here with you while you decide if you want a dog or another cat."

"You have a dog?" I don't know why I'm stunned by this piece of information.

"Yeah, had him for six years now. Got him as a pup when I was still in the military."

"He's staying with your parents?"

"I haven't been home much the last few days," he says, not saying out loud that he hasn't been home much because he's been basically taking care of me since I was released from the hospital. "As good as Maxim is being on his own, I don't like him to be alone, not for long periods of time. He does better when he's around people who don't mind giving him attention."

"He can stay with me," I say immediately, and he grins. "The small yard in the back of the house is fenced in, so he has a place to roam, and I can come home during the day to let him out if I need to."

"He's housebroken; he can hold it." His eyes smile. "I will warn you—he sleeps in my bed when he's with me, and from what my mom and dad have said, he sleeps with them too. He's not a small dog. He hogs the covers and he snores."

"I don't mind. I sleep with light and a sound machine, so his snoring will be like a new form of white noise."

"All right, I'll get him from my parents tomorrow and bring him over so you two can meet. If things work out, he can stay with you for the time being. I'll also give your landlord the deposit, since you'll actually be helping me out."

"You don't have to do that," I deny with a shake of my head. "I would end up paying the deposit anyway, and plus, having him around will give me an idea of if I'm cut out to be a dog owner."

"Now that Maxim is an adult, he's easy. When he was a pup it was a different story. He was into everything and had no idea of his size or the damage he could do. I can't even tell you the number of times I came home when he was a puppy to find that he somehow escaped from his kennel and mauled the garbage, dragging it all over the house."

"Maybe I'm not cut out for owning a dog," I murmur, and he grins.

"He doesn't do that kind of thing anymore, but still, if you do decide to get a puppy, that kind of thing is unavoidable until they are older and trained."

"Good to know," I say, and he tugs me over then kisses me softly with a smile on his lips. Just as the kiss is starting to get heated, the doorbell rings, announcing our food has arrived.

We eat watching TV in comfortable silence, and when we've both finished, we clean up then head for my room without a word of where he's sleeping. Like we have been doing it for years, we work in sync, each of us using the bathroom to change and brush our teeth before getting into bed.

"Thanks for dinner," I tell him as he pulls me into his side.

"Anytime."

"Also, thanks for being here for me these last few days." He doesn't say a word to that, but his arm around my shoulders tightens, forcing me closer to his chest, then he places a kiss to the top of my head. "Night, Cobi."

"Sweet dreams, baby." My eyes close, and before I know it, I fall asleep, having nothing but sweet dreams.

Hadley — Cobi

Cobi

Chapter 8

MY EYES OPEN AND I turn to look at the clock on the side of the bed. It's not even three in the morning, way too early for me to be awake. Not sure what woke me, I tip my head down to look at Hadley. She's sleeping soundly with her head on my chest, one thigh cocked and resting over the top of mine, and her arm across my stomach. I start to close my eyes then hear a noise that seems out of place. I lie still and wait to see if I hear the sound again.

When wood creaks and what sounds like soft footsteps registers, I carefully dislodge Hadley and get out of bed. I feel for my gun on the nightstand and close my eyes when I remember leaving it locked in my truck in the gun safe under my seat. I didn't want to scare Hadley by bringing it into the house; I didn't want the visual of my weapon to bring up memories for her.

I make it to the bedroom door and open it slowly. The living room and kitchen are dark, the only light coming from the clock on the microwave. I scan the room then pause when I see a dark shadow shift slightly. Adrenalin starts to pump through my veins as I wait, holding my breath. When the shadow doesn't move again, I open the door and move toward the light switch just off the kitchen. As soon as I flip the light on, a dark figure wearing a hoodie rushes past me toward the front door. I give chase, but before I can catch up, the person opens the door and disappears outside.

When I get to the door, I stop. No way in hell am I leaving Hadley unprotected. I watch them run down the block, keeping to the shadows. I close and lock the door then go to the bedroom and grab my cell. I call dispatch and inform them of the break-in. During the call, Hadley wakes up and stares at me with wide eyes as I relay into the phone that someone was in the house and that they got away before I could apprehend them.

"Get dressed, baby," I tell her once I hang up and turn on the light. "Officers are on their way."

"Someone was in the house?" she asks, pulling the blankets up over her lap and looking toward the living room with fear in her eyes.

I get closer to her and place my hand against her cheek, dragging her attention to me. "They're gone. You're safe."

"Someone was in the house?" she repeats, staring into my eyes. "Did you see who it was?"

"No." My jaw clenches.

Her eyes close and she drops her head forward. "He wouldn't," she whispers, catching me off guard, and I frown.

"What?"

"Was anything taken?" She looks up at me.

"I haven't had a chance to look around. If they did take something, it was small enough for them to carry without me noticing."

She nods then tosses back the blankets and gets up off the bed. I start to open my mouth to ask what she's doing, but stop when I see she's on a mission. I follow behind her then freeze as she picks up her purse and dumps the contents out on the top of the island. "My wallet." She looks at me. "My wallet is gone."

"Anything else?" I look around and she does the same, leaving the island and walking around the room. Nothing seems out of place, but I haven't been here enough to know exactly where everything is.

"I don't think anything else is gone." She shakes her head. "I... I think I know who did this."

"Who?" I growl, and she bites her bottom lip while wrapping her arms around her waist.

"My dad."

I blink in surprise. I must have heard her wrong. "Excuse me?"

"My dad. I think...." She shakes her head and looks away. "Yesterday, he asked if I could help him and my mom with their electric bill. I told him no."

"You think your father broke into your house in the middle of the night to steal from you, even after what happened to you days ago?" My words are spoken through clenched teeth and anger starts to fill every cell in my body. What kind of man would do that to his child, especially after what she just went through?

"I...." she starts, but stops when there is a knock on the door.

"Get dressed," I order softly, turning away from her. I don't want to make her feel any worse than she already does. I don't want her to see how pissed off I am.

"Cobi."

When my gaze meets hers, the anger I'm feeling is amplified. Her eyes glistening is my undoing, and I swear to God I'm going to kill her dad if I find out it was him who broke in. I move toward her, calling, "Hold on," to the officers outside. Once I'm close, I wrap my hand around the side of her neck and gentle my voice. "Get dressed and come right back out to me. It's going to be all okay, sweetheart."

"Cobi."

"I promise you, baby, it's going to be okay." I bend my head down and kiss her wobbling bottom lip then pull back to look into her eyes once more. "Do what I asked and come back to me."

"Okay," she whispers, and I let her go, watching her as she disappears into the bedroom.

I pull in a few breaths before going to the door and opening it. I let Haws and Tracy, two officers I know, into the house, shaking their hands. I've worked with each of them a few times in the past, and both are good people and officers, having been with the local PD for years. While Hadley is getting dressed, I relay the story of what happened to them, tell them how I woke up and heard a sound, then went in search of it and saw someone run from the house. I tell them I didn't get a glimpse of him or her, but in my estimation, the person was a man, the height alone leading me to believe that fact. They must have been at least six foot, and not many women are that tall. I tell them about Hadley mentioning that it might have been her father who broke in, and when Hadley comes out of the bedroom dressed, they ask her what her father's name is. I'm stunned that I know of him. I've personally never dealt with Derrick Emmerson, but his name and his wife's have come up in meetings more than once since I started with the department.

"I don't know for sure if it was him," Hadley says, and I pull her against me, rubbing her arm when her voice cracks. "But he asked me just yesterday to borrow money, and he knows I always keep at least a hundred dollars cash in my wallet." She shakes her head. "He's the only person I can think of who'd break in."

Not liking the idea of her believing her father would do this to her, I ask, "Do you guys know if any other break-ins have happened in the area?" Looking between both officers, I watch as they share a look then shake their heads.

"None in this neighborhood, but the days are getting shorter and the holidays are coming up. People always start getting desperate around this time of year," Tracy says, and I nod. Hadley's neighborhood is one of the safer ones within the city limits, but Tracy is right. With the holidays fast approaching, break-ins are occurring more and more. Most people will get a second job to provide for their family, but there are some who will just go out and take from others in order to give their loved ones what they think they need. I can't even tell you the number of times I've been called to a home in the month of December with the owners telling me that someone stole all the gifts from under their tree or packages off their doorstep. Christmas makes people crazy, and the crime rate during the holidays is proof of that.

"Do you know how they got in?" Haws questions.

"I haven't done a sweep yet. Didn't want to go out without my weapon, which is locked up in my truck."

"I'm going to check around the house to see if I can find an entry point," he mumbles before giving out chin lifts and heading outside.

"Did you notice anything telling about the perpetrator before they took off?" Tracy asks.

"Nothing more than what I already told you. I'm not sure if they wore a mask, but I didn't see their face. I couldn't even tell if they were Caucasian."

"What direction did they head in?"

"Toward 5th Street. I lost sight of them when they got to the end of the block." My hand clenches in frustration. "I didn't pursue them after they took off. I didn't want to leave Hadley alone, and like I said before, I had no gun."

"Probably smart you let them go," Tracy says, while Hadley nuzzles my chest with the side of her face. I kiss the top of her head and try to force myself to relax when I feel how tense she is. I don't want her to feel my anger and feed off it, especially not in the middle of the night. She still has a few hours to sleep, and I want her to do that without having another nightmare.

"Do you need anything else from Hadley?" I ask, and Tracy's eyes go to her and soften.

"Just one more thing," Tracy says, and I brace, seeing the look in her eyes. "Under normal circumstances, I would not ask, but if we find out it was your dad who broke in, how do you want us to proceed?"

Fuck.

Hadley's entire body gets tight, and I feel every muscle in contact with me bunch as her breath hitches.

"Tracy," I warn, and her eyes meet mine.

"I think I need to ask, Mayson, due to the circumstances."

"If my dad did this, I want you to move forward however you normally would," Hadley says in a quiet voice, ending my stare down with Tracy.

"Are you sure about that, baby?" I question, capturing her chin between my fingers to force her to look me in the eyes. I know from our previous conversations that her parents are a sore subject, but I have no idea of their current relationship.

"I'm sure," she whispers.

When I catch a glimpse of the tears in her eyes, I turn her into me and hold the back of her head, placing her face against my neck. "Are we finished?" I ask Tracy.

"Yeah, if we need anything else, I'll call you tomorrow."

"Thanks." I follow her to the door with Hadley still tucked against my front, and Tracy gives me an apologetic look before she leaves. Once she's gone, I lock the door and lead Hadley to the bedroom. I get into bed with her and bite back a curse when her tears soak through my tee.

"Talk to me, Hadley. Tell me what you're thinking."

"It was him. I know it was him," she whimpers, burrowing into my side.

"Baby." I roll into her and tighten my arms around her small frame.

Her body goes solid immediately and she tries to pull away. "This can't happen."

"What?"

"Let me go." She struggles without answering.

I don't let go. I hold her tighter and place my mouth to her ear. "I'm not letting you go, Hadley."

"You have to." She tries to get free, but she's no match for me. I'm stronger and more determined than she is. "You have to let me go. Please, just let me go," she whimpers as the fight leaves her body.

"Never," I state, holding my lips to the top of her head. "I'm never letting you go." It's a vow. I couldn't let her go even if I wanted to. With every second I spend with her, I understand more and more that she was made for me. When her body stills and her breath evens out, I look down at her face. Her eyes are closed, but I know she's not asleep. "You're mine, Hadley, mine until I take my last breath."

Her muscles bunch in response to my confession, proving she's awake, but she doesn't open her mouth to reply.

One thing I know for certain—this will be the last night she stays here. Even if I have to tie her to my bed, she will be staying at my place with me protecting her until I know without a doubt she's safe.

I wait until I know she's sleeping before I close my eyes, but even then, I don't fall asleep. I can't. The sun will rise like it always does, and I know when that happens, I will have a whole new fight on my hands.

"Is this your new plan?" I ask, leaning against the counter across from Hadley. I hide my smile with my cup of coffee when she doesn't say anything, doesn't even acknowledge me. She's been ignoring me all morning. As soon as she woke up, she rolled out of my arms and out of bed without a backward glance. Since then, she's pretended I don't even exist. "I'm going to be working tonight, but I'll make sure you get settled in at my place before I have to take off." That gets a reaction; her head swings my way and her eyes narrow. "I'm not letting you stay here alone." I shrug. "At least not until I find out if your dad was the one who broke in." I finish my cup of coffee and dump my mug in the sink. She's still staring at me, and I can see the wheels in her head spinning, trying to figure out what she should do. "I gotta go."

When I see the relieved look in her eyes, I almost smile. I go around the counter to where she's sitting and lift her ass right out of her chair, listening to her squeak as I set her on top of the island. With my hands behind her knees, I spread her legs then grab her ass and pull her flush against me. Her breath catches and my cock aches. When her hands move to my chest, I bury my fingers in her hair, tip her head back, and kiss her.

She doesn't fight the kiss, doesn't even attempt to deny me entry. She opens her mouth under mine and moans when our tongues touch. Fuck, I love the way she tastes, love the sounds she makes and the way she can't seem to get close enough to me when we're like this. Not wanting to but knowing I have to, I drag my mouth from hers. "Sorry, baby, I gotta go."

"Okay," she pants against my lips.

"In order for me to do that, I'm gonna need you to let me go," I say, and she drops her head forward, unhooks her legs from around my hips, and releases the hold she has on my shirt. When she keeps her head down, I force her to look at me and grin. "I'll see you tonight."

"Cobi."

"I know you have dinner plans with Brie this evening, so call me when you're on your way home from that. I'll meet you here before you follow me to my place and we get you settled there."

"I'm not staying at your place."

"You're not staying here. This place is no longer safe. I need to focus when I'm working tonight and I won't be able to do that if I'm thinking about how I'm unable to protect you when I'm not here. My house has a state of the art security system, along with Maxim, who would let you know if someone he didn't know was in the house, and then attack them for being in his space."

"How about I stay with Brie and Kenyon then."

"And if you have a nightmare?" She looks past my shoulder and presses her lips together. She doesn't want to admit it, but she knows no one keeps her bad dreams away but me. "You could just tell me why you're once again trying to push me away. We could talk about it then you could give in and stay with me."

"You said you're working tonight. You won't even be home."

"Talk to me."

"There is nothing to talk about."

"So fucking stubborn." I grab both sides of her face so I have her complete attention. "If this is about your dad, you need to know I don't give a fuck who your parents are."

"My parents?" she whispers, and I rub my thumbs along her jaw.

"Baby, I know exactly who your mom and dad are. I haven't ever personally dealt with them, but I know the kind of people they are. I also know that doesn't reflect on you. You are not them."

"We can't do this."

"We're already doing it. I told you before, and I'll keep telling you until you understand. You're mine and I'm not letting you go."

"I'm not yours."

"You are."

"I'm not an object you can own, Cobi, and I don't want to be owned. Ever."

"Whatever." I lean in and kiss her nose. "I gotta go. I'll see you this evening."

"I just told you I'm not—"

I cut her off, dropping a quick kiss to her lips before picking up my duffle bag. "I'll call Brie as soon as I leave to let her know the plan."

"You can't just call my best friend," she snaps, as she hops off the counter and starts to follow me to the door.

"Have a good day, baby." I open the door and walk out onto the porch, laughing as she shouts about me being an overbearing ass. When I get into my truck, I smile at her as she glares at me.

When she spins around and slams the door, I know I'm already halfway in love with her.

I open the door to my truck and get out, with Maxim hopping out behind me. I know Hadley's home; her car is in the drive along with another one. Figuring Brie is inside, I head up to the front door and use my key to get in. Both women turn to look at me—Brie with a bright smile, Hadley with a frown.

"I see we need to have another conversation about my key," she states, and I grin at her then watch a smile spread across her full lips when she spots Maxim at my side. She slides off the stool she's sitting on and gets closer to Maxim, holding out her hand.

"Hey, handsome." She gets down to eye level with him, running her fingers over the top of his head, and then laughs as he starts to lick her face.

"Can I get a hello kiss?" I ask, and she looks up at me.

"No."

"It wasn't really a question." I smile then pull her up against me, listening to her squeak right before I capture her mouth.

When I pull away, her breathless "Brie's here" makes me laugh.

"Please, don't mind me," Brie says, and I look to find her giving Maxim a belly rub.

"How was dinner?"

"Good," Brie answers. "I'm sure your ears were burning."

At her statement, I smile down at Hadley, who's a pretty shade of pink, then ask, "Did you pack your bag?"

"I'm going to stay with Brie."

"You're not," I deny.

"She knows she's not staying with us." Brie narrows her eyes at Hadley. "We already talked about it. She knows she's better off staying with you; she's just being hardheaded."

"You mean *you* talked about it," Hadley says, taking a step away from me and turning to face her friend.

"Okay, I talked about it and know that even if you're too stubborn to admit it, you know I'm right. Do you need me to help you pack?"

"No." Hadley denies looking annoyed.

"All right, then I'm gonna head home." Brie grabs her purse and gives me a wink then Hadley a hug.

When she's gone, I look at Hadley. "I went and talked to your dad today." At my statement, her body freezes. "He's adamant that he had nothing to do with what happened last night. He said he was home with your mom and she could confirm that if I needed her to." I pull in a breath and grab her hand, dragging her up against me. "He was concerned about you. Said he didn't like the idea of you being here on your own, even after I told him that you and I are together."

"I'm sure he was worried," she mumbles, rolling her eyes.

Not wanting to upset her right now by digging into her relationship with her parents, I change the subject. "Did you call your bank and credit cards?"

"Yeah, they're all canceled. I still have to get to the DMV for a new license, but that will have to wait until tomorrow after I meet with one of my clients."

"Anything I can help with?"

Her face softens and she shakes her head. "No, but thank you."

I kiss the top of her head and release her. "Go pack. I want time to show you around my place before I gotta leave for work."

"Cobi—"

"I'm not arguing with you about this again. Go pack."

"Maybe I need my head examined," she huffs, before turning away and going to her room.

I listen to her talking to herself and the sound of banging then look at Maxim, who's lying on the floor near the couch. "What do you think, bud?" He barks at me then gets up and heads into her bedroom, giving me his answer, and I smile.

Hadley

Chapter 9

I HEAR THE GARAGE door go up, and Maxim, who knows his dad is home, lifts his head off my stomach but otherwise doesn't move. A minute later, I listen to the door open, the sound of heavy boots on the wood floors, and then the sound of keys hitting the countertop in the kitchen. When the bedroom door opens a couple of seconds later, I peek through my lashes and watch Cobi move quietly through the room. Maxim finally gets up and his tags rattle as Cobi talks quietly to him. After a few minutes he goes into the bathroom, shutting the door before turning on the light and Maxim leaves the bedroom, probably to sleep on the couch.

I squeeze my eyes shut when the shower goes on and visions of a naked Cobi fill my mind. Wide-awake with my body buzzing, my nipples tingling, and the space between my thighs hot, I pray for a miracle. This is what hell must be like, having something you want close but just out of reach. When the shower shuts off and he comes out of the bathroom, I open my eyes just enough to see him wearing nothing but a pair of sleep pants that hang low on his hips, accentuating the deep V of his abdomen and his tattoos, tattoos that make him look even more intense. I close my eyes once more and pretend to sleep while he gets into bed with me.

When he rolls me over and pulls me against his warm, clean-smelling chest, I almost whimper and beg him to have his way with me.

"You asleep, baby?"

I don't answer him. I lay as still as possible, hoping the throbbing between my legs will go away. Throbbing that started because of the book I was reading then got worse when I got into his bed and surrounded myself with his scent. I thought about masturbating, but I couldn't bring myself to do it.

When his hand slides slowly down my back, over my simple cotton nightgown and comes to rest on one cheek of my ass, my heartbeat picks up. "Hadley." His warm breath skims across the shell of my ear and a shiver slides across my skin. He moves his hand lower down the back of my thigh then back up, under my nightgown, over my ass and lace panties. "Fuck." That one word is filled with hunger as his hips jerk forward, sending his hard cock into my belly.

A whimper I can no longer control escapes, and my hand wraps around his bicep to hold on. Before I can even pull in another breath he rolls me to my back and settles himself between my thighs. The new position sends my heart rate higher and my head spinning. Without a word spoken between us, I lean up as he drops his head forward and our mouths meet. The kiss is frantic and uncontrolled, as we bite, lick, and nip at each other's mouths.

When he pulls his mouth from mine and kisses down my neck, I arch into him then moan as he pulls down the top of my nightgown and takes my breast into his mouth. Sucking hard, he circles my nipple before biting down on the tight bud. I wrap my legs around him and grind against his hardness. He switches to my other breast while his hand moves down my side, and then he slips his hand in my panties and rolls his fingers over my clit, making me cry out.

"Christ, Hadley, you're fucking soaked, baby." He slips two fingers inside me and nips my other breast, before muttering, "So fucking wet and soft."

"I need you," I beg. "Please, I need you." With a groan, he rubs his fingers against my G-spot then pulls his hand from me. He shoves my panties to the side then he's inside me, filling me up in one quick, harsh thrust that is painfully perfect.

God he's big, so big it almost hurts to take him as he starts to pound his hips into mine. I slide my legs down to wrap around the back of his thighs then lift my hands over my head, placing them against the headboard as he rides me hard and fast. When his fingers find my clit again, I make a noise I've never made before, crying out as an unexpected orgasm rushes over me, sending my mind into darkness. My body shakes and my pussy convulses around his hard cock. Never, never have I felt anything like what I'm feeling as he rides me through my orgasm. When I come down from my climax, I focus on his face above mine and lift my hands to his jaw, sliding my fingers along the scruff on his cheeks.

"I need to feel all of you," he says, pulling out of me suddenly and stripping me of my clothes then removing his own. When he enters me again and his warm, hard body settles over mine, I close my eyes. I have never felt more connected to another person than I do right now. I have never felt more complete. I wrap myself around him and bury my face in his neck, not wanting him to read the look on my face or to see the tears I feel gathering in my eyes.

"Fucking look at me, Hadley." His harsh words force my head back and I meet his gaze. When our eyes lock, he brings his hand up to rest against my cheek then he closes his eyes, slowing his thrusts. When his eyes open, I stare into them as he kisses me again. He stops moving and rests his weight on me as my heart thunders in my chest. This kiss is different than the others we've shared. I know without words he's telling me that I'm his, and that he's never letting me go.

With his mouth locked on mine, his hips start a slow, torturous circle, his cock hitting a spot inside me over and over in a slow tempo while his mouth devours mine. Our eyes stay locked as another orgasm starts to build within me, making my stomach muscles bunch and my hands on his shoulders tighten. I feel him get even bigger and know the exact moment he comes, because his orgasm sets mine off. I slide my hands into his hair and keep his mouth fused against mine as we ride out the wave of pleasure that has enveloped us both. When he drags his mouth from mine and rests his head in the crook of my neck, I wonder if he knows he's ruined me forever.

"You okay?" he asks, leaning back to look at me and capturing my face between his palms. Still breathing heavily, I jerk my head up and down in a silent yes. He smiles, kisses my lips, and then rolls us to the side. As he slides out of me, I let out a small whimper. "Did I hurt you?"

"No." I rub my face against his chest while my arms around him tighten. "Not at all."

"You know what this means, right?" At his question, my muscles bunch and my lungs stop working. "I'm never letting you go, Hadley. I might have been able to do it before you gave yourself to me in this bed, but there is no way I could do it now."

I close my eyes as tears threaten to spill from between my lashes.

The truth is, I want to believe he wants me.

All of me.

I just don't know if I can trust him. I don't know him well enough to trust he's being honest when he says he wants me for more than just this moment. Having the childhood I did, I learned at an early age that actions speak louder than words, that just because someone says they care for you doesn't mean they do, and that just because someone is supposed to love you doesn't mean they will. My parents taught me that harsh lesson early on in life.

"You're mine. I know you don't get that yet, but I promise you, baby, there is nowhere safer for you to be than with me."

"I always feel safe when I'm with you," I admit before I can think better of it, and his arms around me pull me impossibly closer to him.

"That's because you are safe," he says, each softly spoken word brushing against my forehead where his lips are resting.

"Be patient with me."

"Promise," he agrees quietly.

I close my eyes and hold onto him. I don't tell him that I don't know how to trust him, that I don't even know what love is. I don't tell him that the two people in this world who should have shown me never did. I want to open up to him about my past, but instead, I press my lips together and fight back tears, refusing to give into them.

I press my nose into his chest and breathe in his scent. Eventually, I fall asleep in his arms, cocooned in warmth, feeling safe like I always do when he's near me.

I smell the scent of bacon and my stomach rumbles before I even open my eyes. I sit up in bed and look around then down at myself. I'm still completely naked, my nightgown and panties nowhere in sight. After searching through the tangled blanket and sheet, I find both items of clothing and get up out of bed, slipping them on. With the door open, I can hear Cobi in the kitchen and the television on as I go to the bathroom to brush my teeth.

After I splash some cool water on my face, I look at my reflection in the mirror. I look different. I don't know if it's what happened last night or what has happened over the last few days, but I don't look like my old self. The look in my eyes seems more sedated, and I feel more secure in who I am.

When I head out of the bathroom, I'm greeted by Maxim, who leans into my side. I scratch him behind his ears, and his big brown doggie eyes meet mine. He's adorable, and I had no choice but to fall in love with him since the moment we met.

"Come on." I run my fingers through the fur on the top of his head one more time then go into the main living area of Cobi's townhouse. I once again let out an uncomfortable sigh as I head for the kitchen. Cobi's place is awesome, with a view of rolling hills out his kitchen window and a small manmade lake just outside a sliding door and back deck. His place is two stories, the garage and storage on the main floor then upstairs is the living area, two bedrooms, two and a half baths and an open floor plan. The unit is new, as in it was only built a few months ago. It's in a part of town that is only now being built up with grocery stores, coffee shops, and fast food restaurants.

As I head through his living room with Maxim on my heels, I'm overwhelmed by the beauty of the open space. His brightly lit kitchen with white cabinets and speckled granite is open to the living room, the large space broken up with a long peninsula that has three barstools lining the edge. He has a wide-seated, dark gray, brushed leather couch in front of a state-of-the-art entertainment center, complete with a sixty-inch flat screen TV. Built-in shelves line one of the walls, and decorative wallpaper in silvers and golds accent the open space, making it feel cozier.

When I reach the kitchen, I stop to take in a bare-chested Cobi in front of the stove, flipping over bacon in a pan. My body tingles and my mouth waters as I study him. Seriously, he's the hottest and most intense man I have ever met in my life. I can't believe that just last night I had all of his power on me and in me, filling me with something unexpected and memorable. Even just standing in his kitchen, he's mesmerizing; I could watch him for hours and constantly come up with something new I like about him. It doesn't help that he's not just hot, but he's sweet and caring—something that is a rare quality in men these days.

"Morning, baby," he says, turning to look at me as I lean against the wall at the edge of the kitchen, needing it to hold me up, unsure if I can keep my feet under me. Maxim, who is still at my side, rests his heavy head against my thigh, and I run my hand over his fur and scratch behind his ears.

"Morning," I whisper, and he smiles just slightly, his lips barely tipping up at the corners.

"I'm trying really fucking hard not to be jealous of my dog, baby. Maybe you wanna help me out with that by coming to kiss your man?"

My man?

I couldn't even fathom a man like Cobi a week ago. I would never even have dared to dream up a guy like him, so it's seriously difficult for me to think about him being mine.

"Babe." The one word is impatient, causing me to jump in place. I move from the wall and head toward him. As soon as I'm within touching distance, he wraps his hand around my hip and pulls me flush against him. I don't lean up to kiss him. I don't have to, because he bends down and captures my mouth in a searing kiss that makes my toes curl and body buzz. When he releases me, his eyes search mine. "No dreams last night?"

"No." I shake my head, running my hands up his biceps and over his tattoos.

"You still need to keep going. Even if the dreams stop for a time, you need to talk things out."

"I have an appointment tomorrow."

He kisses my forehead in approval. "Want some coffee?"

"Yes, please," I say, and he keeps me attached to him with his arm around my waist as he leads me to the coffee pot and pulls down a cup from the cupboard above. He pours me a cup of coffee then fixes it for me just how I like it.

"Sit with me while I finish up breakfast." It's not a request; it's an order, and I know this when he lifts me up and plants my ass on the cold counter. I sit and sip my coffee while he finishes up the bacon then he uses the bacon grease to fry the eggs. When he pulls out a loaf of bread, I hop down and take it from him, figuring it would be rude if I didn't even try to help out.

"Do you have to work today?"

"Yep, but not until this evening," he says, meeting my gaze as I press down the lever on the toaster. "I should be home around the same time I was this morning. I have the weekend off though, so I figured either Saturday or Sunday we could go see Harmony. She called me yesterday asking how you're doing."

"How is she?" I ask, feeling like a weight has suddenly settled in the pit of my stomach.

"Good, home now. The media hasn't stopped trying to contact her, so she's laying low for the time being."

"I'm sorry she's dealing with that," I say truthfully. I hated even the idea of having to talk to the media and am thankful I never got caught out where I would have to. I feel like an asshole even thinking it, considering what she must be going through, but I'm relieved they let the story having to do with me go and have left me alone.

"Me too, but I'm also relieved that you don't have to deal with that," he says, reading my mind.

He comes over to where I'm standing and places a kiss against the side of my head, and I look up at him, asking, "Is she really okay?"

"She's got our family and her fiancé protecting her, so she's good.

Not sure she'd be that way if she was on her own."

On her own like me; he doesn't have to say it, but I know that's exactly what he means. Up until Cobi came along, the only people I really had in my life were Brie and Kenyon, and that reminder is a depressing one. Maybe it's time I make some changes. Maybe it's time I make some friends and get a life that doesn't revolve around monthly dates with Brie and reality TV shows. "I'd really like to see her this weekend if she's up to it," I say, feeling more confident.

"I should probably warn you that my mom and dad will likely be there, so you'd also be meeting them."

"Your parents?" I know my eyes are wide with horror. I'm sure I look like a deer caught in a set of bright white headlights with a car coming toward it going fifty miles an hour.

"They will love you, Hadley, so get that look off your face, baby."

"I don't know how to meet parents. Meeting people is even a new thing for me." He laughs, tossing his head back. "I'm not actually being funny."

"I know, babe, but you still are." He touches his mouth to mine. "It's going to be fine. You'll see."

I'm not as sure as he is. Really, I don't think he understands what he's asking me to do. I have never been social. I have always found a way to agree to social gatherings but escape at the last minute without seeming rude. Brie and Kenyon are the only people I spend any real time with, and that's only because I have known them for years.

"If you say so," I murmur, getting another smile from him before he lets me go and heads back to the eggs he's frying.

Having a couple of hours before I have to leave for work, and his place being closer to my job than mine, I eat with him, enjoying the moment before I have to get ready to leave. When the time finally closes down on us and the bubble we've created, I go get ready for work, and afterward he walks me to my car, waiting until I'm inside and pulling away to head back into his townhouse.

"Hadley." The sigh in Reggie's tone lets me know what I already suspect. He's done. He doesn't want to listen to me anymore, and he sure as heck doesn't want to believe what I have been telling him for the last ten minutes.

"Reggie, I'll look into things, but my records show that Marcus received the funds issued to him for his new football uniform. The money was deposited. I don't know what happened afterward, since the money is untraceable on my end after that."

"He never got the money, Hadley. I don't give a fuck what your system says. He never received the money, and now me and Shawna are paying for his uniform out of pocket. I don't mind doing that, because he's my kid, but still, that money is his. He should have had it, and now he doesn't."

Marcus, who is now fifteen, has been with the Shill family for three years. His biological mother has been in and out of rehab and court so many times I've lost count. She is in a constant battle to get herself together, but has yet to succeed in her endeavors.

"I promise you I'll look into things," I say, and Reggie sighs once more. "I'll call you as soon as I learn anything new."

"Thanks, Hadley. I know this isn't your fuck up, but shit like this can't go on. It's not fair to Marcus. If this were another kid and they didn't have people like Shawna and me to help pay for the extra stuff, they'd be fucked."

"I know," I agree softly. "We'll talk soon." I hang up after saying goodbye, feeling guilty. I look at my computer monitor once more. The reason for the money being dealt out is right there in black and white, along with the check being received and cashed.

Thinking about what Marian said, about funds going missing, I get up and head for her office after turning off my computer. The door is closed, so I knock, and like normal, Marian doesn't immediately say to come in. After what feels like five minutes, she finally calls out to me and I push inside. She's sitting at her desk, her dark hair pulled away from her face in a harsh bun, her makeup perfectly in place and her suit unwrinkled. If she weren't pretty, I'd say she looked like the evil principal from *Matilda*, but unfortunately, she's pretty. I take a seat across from her and she raises an annoyed brow, barely glancing away from her computer.

"How can I assist you, Miss Emmerson?"

Instead of saying, *"You can help me and everyone else who works here by not being such an evil cow,"* I launch into what happened with Marcus. When I'm finished, she gives me nothing, nothing helpful anyway.

She tells me that Marcus must be lying and that he probably lied to his family about getting the money and spending it. I might have believed her with one of the other kids, but Marcus has been happy since he's been with the Shill family. He's taken on his role as big brother to two other foster kids with pride, has been present at school, and is getting better grades. I know from talking to him and his foster family that he loves to play football, something that without the money he would not be able to do, since it's an extra expense that most foster families aren't willing to cover.

Before I leave her office, she tells me to let things go and that she will look into it. Not feeling good about her response, I send an email to the company who overlooks the funds allotted to the kids. I hope they will be able to help me sort this mess out, that someone will actually care enough to really look into things.

Chapter 10

I WATCH COBI GIVE me a smile as he backs out of his garage, and I give him an awkward smile in return. When his turns into a grin, I roll my eyes, which makes him laugh. When the garage door finally closes, cutting off my view of him, I look down at Maxim, who's leaning into my side, and scratch him behind his ears.

"I guess it's just us for the night, big guy. Come on." I head back upstairs into the main living area of Cobi's townhouse and go right to the kitchen. I pour myself a glass of wine and then lean back against the counter, watching the news Cobi left playing on the excessively large TV across the room.

Normally, I never watch the news. It's depressing, especially with so many political debates going on right now, but Cobi seems to always be watching it when he's home. I'm sure it's ingrained in him because he's a police officer and is required to know what is going on in the world around him. Me, on the other hand? I prefer to live with my head in the sand until it's time to vote.

When my cell phone on the counter rings, I check the caller ID. I see it's my father calling… again, for the third time in as many days, and deny the call. I know my dad is calling because he's worried about my relationship with Cobi. He's just not worried for the normal reasons a father would be. He's worried that I will talk to Cobi about my past, about the things I know my dad does to make money and about my mom. Regardless of what he said to Cobi, I'm sure it was him who broke into my place, especially after finding out that only my wallet was taken. Cobi doesn't know my dad, so he doesn't know his concern for my safety was just a farce, a way of him appearing like he actually cares for me when he doesn't—something he's done since I was a little girl.

After another sip of wine, I take my glass with me toward the bedroom to grab the book I've been reading the last few days. Cobi and I were supposed to be home together tonight, and we made plans this morning to go to dinner at my favorite sushi place. But not even ten minutes after I got to his place, he got a call that he had to get to work. I didn't ask him what happened but did tell him that I hoped everything was okay after he kissed me goodbye at the door to his truck and gave Maxim a head rub.

With a sigh, I shake my head. Even though he just left, I already miss him. Over the last few days of staying with him, my walls have crumbled down around my feet, burying me deeper under the feel of contentment I get whenever we're together. Who could blame me? It would be impossible for anyone to spend time with him without falling for him. There is a connection between us, something I have never felt before with another person. He makes me happy, makes me laugh, and he makes me forget where I came from. When we're together, I can pretend that nothing else matters but him and me and the relationship we are building.

Hearing my cell ring again, I go back toward the kitchen and smile as I put it to my ear, answering, "Hello."

"Cobi called. He told me he has to work, so I should come keep you company," Brie says, and I fight back laughter. Somehow, Cobi and her have become allies over the last week and Cobi has used his persuasive abilities to get Brie on his side in the fight to convince me that we are meant to be together. Something he no longer needs to do.

"He just left—" I look at the clock. "—not even fifteen minutes ago." I try to sound annoyed, even though I'm not.

"I know. Anyway, I'm calling to let you know I'm on my way. I should be there in less than twenty. Do you need anything?"

"Wine," I respond before taking another sip from my glass.

"That bad?"

No, that good, I think with a short shake of my head. "No, I just haven't had time to get to the store and I just poured my last glass from the bottle Cobi bought me."

"I love him. I'll stop on my way." I hear the smile in her voice and I let out a sigh. "I don't know how you're annoyed when you're living with Cobi Mayson. Seriously, you should be on cloud nine."

"I'm not annoyed; I'm just rethinking our friendship. I'm starting to believe you're more loyal to Cobi than you are to me."

"I'm not even going to get into this over the phone." She laughs. "I'll talk to you when I get there. By the way, I'm bringing all my wedding stuff." She hangs up before I can respond.

Dropping my phone to the counter, I look at Maxim, who appears at my side. "How about I feed you before Brie gets here?" He barks in response then lies down on the tiled kitchen floor with a groan, waiting for me to serve him. I fill his bowl with a mixture of dry and wet food then head toward Cobi's bedroom. His king-sized bed is still like we left it this morning after we made love and finally got up. The deep brown feather duvet is half hanging off the bed and the sheets are wrinkled and twisted into a knot. I make the bed haphazardly and toss on the pillows before I head for the closet to change out of my work clothes.

When Brie arrives thirty minutes later, she's carrying a box of wine and a bag I can see is overflowing with magazines and her wedding planner.

"You got me a box of wine." I smile, taking it from her, and she rolls her eyes.

"You've been drinking the same thing since we were in college. I used to think it was because we were in college and way too poor to afford anything better. I know now you just like cheap wine."

"It tastes good," I counter. "And it has thirty-four glasses in it, which means I basically have an endless supply of wine when the mood to drink strikes."

"Whatever you say, babe, but I'm sure those people from Napa Valley would stone you to death if they ever heard you say that wine from a box tastes good."

"It does taste good." I take the box to the fridge and set it inside. "Do you want something to drink?"

"I brought myself a small bottle of amaretto, and I told Kenyon that I'm drinking and that he's going to have to pick me up."

"Works for me," I say as she places her bag on the counter and begins to pull out stuff. She's been working on this wedding since the day Kenyon proposed to her. Literally the day he asked her, she bought a wedding planner and magazines. A week after he asked her, she booked their venue and made an appointment with Julie's, a local baker, to design her wedding cake. The wedding is still six months away, and Kenyon only asked her to marry him four months ago. Still, most of the details have been taken care of due to Brie's excitement and serious planning skills.

"We have a few things to go over tonight, like your bridesmaid dress and who is going to be sitting next to who at the reception. You know I don't get along with most of my family, but still I'm inviting them, partly to rub it in their faces that I got a good man and they didn't play any part in it."

"Honey, I still don't know if it's a good idea that you invite everyone. I think you should just have the people around you who really care about you and your happiness."

"No." She shakes her head and looks at me. "My parents would have wanted them all there, and I want them to know that what they pulled after my parents died didn't break me."

What they did being that they took away the house her parents owned. Her mom and dad never updated their wills, so the property was left to her aunts, two women who should have known better than to take the money that should have been their niece's. They did take it though, and then they used it to help their own children, not giving even a penny to Brie.

"Please don't ask me to be nice to them. I swear, Brie, I don't know if I can do it."

"It's just one day. We can all be nice for one day," she says, sounding sure, but the expression she gives me says otherwise.

"What does Kenyon say about this?"

"That he loves me and he supports my decision."

I stare at her in disbelief. That doesn't sound like Kenyon at all. Yes, he loves Brie, and yes, he's always supportive, but I know he hates her family and has never given up an opportunity to let them know how he feels. "Now what's the truth?"

Huffing, she shakes her head in frustration. "He's not happy about them coming, but he gets why I want them there." I watch her smirk. "He has warned me that if they do anything he doesn't like, not even I will be able to hold him back."

"I hope they don't do anything, even if it would be fun watching Kenyon kick their bottoms out of the venue." As I listen to her laugh, I start searching through the cupboards for something to make us for dinner. Not finding anything, I glance at Brie.

"Do you want to order something in?"

Her head tips to the side. "Cobi said he ordered dinner for us." I blink at her. "Sushi, and sweet and sour chicken."

"I think I'm in love with him," I whisper, and she grins. "No, I'm serious, Brie. How is that even possible? I've only known him for a week."

"I knew the moment I saw Kenyon that I wanted to be with him," she says, holding my gaze. "After three dates, I knew I wanted to spend the rest of my life with him, and after the first time we made love, I knew that I loved him in a way that I always would. Sometimes you just know when you meet the person you're meant to be with."

"It's crazy."

"Yep," she agrees. "Crazy scary, crazy awesome, and sometimes just plain crazy."

"Do I tell him?"

She shrugs one shoulder. "I think there is a rule written somewhere that I should tell you to avoid being honest about your feelings so that you don't scare him off. I say you do what you need to do. If you are in love with him and want him to know—" She shrugs again. "—tell him how you feel." She leans closer to me and takes my hand. "I do think you should give this a little more time. I know you don't have a lot of experience in the relationship department, and I don't want you to confuse love with sex, because they are completely separate."

I swallow over the lump that has suddenly formed in my throat. Is that it? Am I feeling this connected to him because we've had sex? When I've had sex in the past, I never felt like I do now, but then again, I've never been chased through the woods by a madman before. Who knows if everything that's happened isn't messing with my head, making me feel things I don't actually feel.

"You're right. I need to give it time before I say anything to him."

"Oh, Lord," Brie says, getting up and coming to stand directly in front of me. "Please tell me you are not doubting that man and your feelings?"

"I'm taking your advice," I reply, and she suddenly wraps her hands around my biceps and begins to shake me hard. "What the heck are you doing?" I shout as I try to get away from her.

"I'm hoping to shake some damn sense into your head. I didn't tell you to start doubting him. I said you need to give this time so you know it's love and not just the fact that you're finally with a good guy and getting some really good sex."

"I know that." I finally pull free from her hold and blow my hair out of my face. "Sheesh, you're crazy." I smooth out my hair.

"I'm not letting you push him away."

"Brie, I might be messed up from my childhood, but I'm not dumb. I know that Cobi is not just a good man, but probably one of the best there is out there." I rest my hands on my hips and pull in a breath. "I'm not sure why he wants me. I don't know that I will ever figure it out, but I'm not going to be the one to convince him that he doesn't, because believe me, I have tried. Right now, all I know is I'm taking one day with him at a time, and settling into us being together." She continues to stare at me, but now with wide eyes. "He has made it clear more than once that who my family is doesn't matter to him, that only how he feels about me matters." I drag in a shaky breath. "I believe him when he says that. And tomorrow I'm probably meeting his parents, and you know me well enough to know that something like that would not happen no matter how into a guy I was before now."

"You really do love him."

"I don't know. Like you pointed out, this could just be really amazing sex and a fucked up situation making me think I feel things I don't."

"No, you're in love."

"Brie."

"Okay, I'll shut up, but I just want to say I love him for you, Hadley." Her arms wrap around me. "You are not wrong; he's a good man, one of the very few left in the world, and I love the way he's taking care of you. You deserve to have someone take care of you for once."

"Don't make me cry."

"As if I could." She laughs then lets me go. "Now I need a drink, we need to talk about wedding crap, and then we need to find a time to get our guys together for dinner," she says as the doorbell rings, and Maxim barks.

"Well, you get your drink while I get dinner, and then we will figure out the rest," I say before I head down to the front door. I take dinner from the driver who informs me everything has already been taken care of, including the tip. I take the bag to the kitchen with my mind on Cobi and the little ways he finds to take care of me even when he's not around. Not really thinking about what I'm doing, I drop the bag of food on the counter then take my cell phone with me to the bedroom and shut the door.

I press the 'Dial' button on Cobi's number and put my phone to my ear.

"Everything okay, baby?" he answers softly before the second ring, and I lean back against the wall, closing my eyes and not speaking, just letting his gentle tone wash through me and the cracks in my heart, filling them up. "Hadley?" The one word is concerned and I open my eyes.

"Sorry... I just... I just wanted to say thank you," I get out over the sudden burst of emotions I'm feeling.

"It's just Brie and dinner, baby," he says quietly.

"It's not," I reply firmly but just as quietly. "My parents never cared if I ate or if I slept. They didn't care if I had a nightmare or even if I brushed my teeth." I shake my head. "Not that you care about that."

"I care about everything having to do with you and your well-being."

"Yes." My eyes close once more. I'm falling in love with him. "I think I'm falling in love with you," I admit without thinking if I should keep my mouth shut or if it's too soon to admit something like that to him.

"Then we're on the same page." His response is immediate and my heart rate increases. "I hate to end this conversation, but my partner's waiting for me, so we'll talk when I get home later. Okay?"

"Of course," I agree as more contentment fills me. "Be safe."

"I always am. Now I just got another reason to do that. Enjoy your dinner and time with Brie."

"I will."

"Later, babe."

"Later, Cobi." I hang up and go back to the kitchen, where Brie is sipping on her drink while pulling dinner from the bag.

"Everything okay?" she asks when she sees me stop at the edge of the kitchen.

"Perfect." I smile, and she stares at me for a moment, studying my face before she grins.

"Don't stop," I whimper to Cobi as he fucks me from behind, doing it hard, so hard the bed is shaking with the force, and it's difficult to stay on my hands planted against the mattress.

"I couldn't stop if I wanted to," he growls, holding tightly to my hips. "Fuck, you feel good." One palm roams over the cheek of my ass then squeezes.

The sensation of his hand on my ass makes me press back into him, a silent urge. I don't know exactly what I want; I just know I want more.

His large palm stills then moves again and lifts away. I almost cry out in aggravation, but instead moan when his hand comes down hard with a heavy smack.

The sting from his palm sends a pulse right to my clit, and my pussy convulses around his length. "Yesss," I hiss, my head flying back along with my hair.

"Jesus." He smacks my ass harder than before, and I come instantly, my arms sliding out in front of me, no longer able to hold my weight up. With my ass in the air, he rides me through my orgasm, his tempo steady and his thrust hard. When my pussy stops pulsing, he pulls me up until I'm on my knees in front of him, one of his arms wrapping around my waist under my breasts and his other hand grabbing mine, lacing our fingers together and sliding them down my stomach. When our fingers roll over my clit, my head falls back to his shoulder and my eyes close.

"Turn your head and give me your mouth, baby," he orders gruffly while he plants himself deep inside me. I tip my head toward him and his mouth opens over mine. When his tongue slips between my lips, I open wider for him to take more. He starts moving his hips again and our fingers between my legs move faster. I know I'm going to come, and I know I won't be able to stop myself from coming with him when he starts to grow even bigger. His pace increases and his breathing turns ragged against my mouth.

"Cobi," I pant when I feel it coming over me, bigger than even before.

"Let go, Hadley baby. Let go." He nips my bottom lip, and I fall over the edge on a gasp. He thrusts three more times before locking his hips against mine, coming deep inside me. I close my eyes and soak in every detail, our chests heaving in unison, his heart beating hard against my back, our bodies slick with sweat, the smell of sex in the air. "Nothing better than being in you, nothing better than being with you, but really fucking nothing better than you getting off on me smacking your ass and you coming on my cock."

I know my face is red when he's finished speaking, and I turn my face into his neck to hide. When his chest starts to shake, I peek up at him to confirm my suspicion that he's laughing.

"I'm not sure I think this is as funny as you do." I frown at him and his face softens.

"I don't think anything we did is funny, baby. I think it's funny that you're open to me, open to anything I want to do when I'm deep inside you and you're in the moment, but the minute I talk about it, you turn an adorable shade of red."

"I'm not used to talking about sex," I mutter. I've never been with someone who wanted to talk about it, and didn't even know people did that kind of thing.

"I see that." He lifts my chin up so he can place a soft kiss against my mouth. He pulls out of me slowly then gets off the bed and picks me up, carrying me to the bathroom before cleaning us both up. When he leads me back to bed, he maneuvers us so we are face-to-face, wrapping his arm over my waist and tossing his leg over both of mine.

"How many relationships have you been in?" he asks as soon as I'm settled in against him.

"Not many, and none of them lasted long," I admit, looking at his throat.

Taking his arm from my waist, he captures my chin and tips my head back. "Why's that?"

"Most of the time, it had to do with me telling them about my parents, or my parents showing up unannounced and making a scene." I drag in a shaky breath. "None of them stuck around long after that."

"Idiots," he says harshly, and I close my eyes.

"You've only met my dad once, and when you did, he was on his best behavior. You've never met my mom; she's the worst."

"I know all about your dad, baby, and your mom. There is no way in hell I'd let them scare me off."

"Yeah, but you're a cop. You're used to dealing with people like them, while most people aren't."

"You are not your parents, Hadley. Your parents do not define the person you are today. I know people who have grown up in shitty situations and let that lead them down shitty paths. That is not you, baby."

"Have you been talking to Brie about this?" I ask.

His chin jerks back and his face gets kind of scary. "No. Anything I want to learn about you, I want to learn *from* you, not from someone else."

"I just said that, because you sound a lot like she does when she's trying to convince me that I shouldn't be ashamed of how I grew up and who my parents are."

"You shouldn't be ashamed. You should be proud that despite them you have made a life for yourself."

"That's what Dr. Sprat says too."

"Maybe you should listen to us instead of the crap those two idiots filled your head with," he says as his eyes go to my forehead, where I had the stitches taken out today. "I don't think you'll have a scar."

"Me neither. Even if I do, I think it will be small."

As he studies my forehead, sliding his thumb over the mark, I watch the intense look on his face, wondering what it's about. I learn as soon as he speaks again. "I wish the scars from your past could just as easily vanish."

"Cobi." His name is filled with pain as it escapes my throat.

"I won't let them hurt you anymore, Hadley. I need you to really understand that." He looks down into my eyes. "I don't know the relationship you have with them. I don't know how you feel about them, but I won't let you near them or them near you if I think they could cause you more pain."

My jaw aches as my teeth clench together and tears I can't control start to fill my eyes. I've never been a crier, but more and more, it's getting harder to control the urge to let those tears loose when he's being sweet and protective. "I don't talk to them much. They really only contact me when they need something from me."

"Do you give them money?" he questions, sounding annoyed at the idea.

"I used to." I drag in a deep breath then let it out while resting my hand against his jaw. "I stopped when it started to become a habit for them to ask me for money every other week, when they knew I got paid. It's difficult enough to take care of myself most months, and if something happens and I need money, I have no one to ask besides Brie. And she and Kenyon don't have extra, with them paying for a wedding and saving for a house."

"Glad you stopped giving in to them."

"Me too, but it still hasn't stopped them from asking me, and it didn't stop my dad from breaking into my house."

"If I find out—"

"You probably never will," I cut him off. "He's stupid, but not that stupid, and even if you did get evidence that he's the one who broke in, it won't matter anyway."

"He'd go to jail, baby."

"Yeah, he'll spend a few days in jail then be out and back to his old ways. Jail doesn't scare him or my mom, and laws don't either. Both of them have seen the inside of a courtroom more than you probably have. For them, it's their normal." I shake my head. "When I tell you my parents are messed up, I mean they are messed up beyond what the normal definition of messed up is."

"I don't know that there is a normal definition of messed up." He smiles.

"Whatever. You get what I'm saying." I yawn.

"Yeah." He folds his arms around me and rests his lips to my forehead for a moment before tucking my head under his chin, and ordering there, "Sleep."

"Only because I wanted to do that anyway," I murmur.

And the last sound I hear before I fall asleep is him laughing, which means I fall asleep with a smile on my face.

Hadley

Cobi

Cobi

Chapter 11

WHEN THE DOORBELL GOES off along with the chime on my cell phone, I roll and look at the clock on my nightstand. Seeing the time, I bite back a curse. It's just nine, and today is the first day I don't have to work and Hadley doesn't either. Our plans for the day are to go see Harmony at some point, but we don't have to do that until this evening. I should be sleeping in, waking with my woman, and then making love to her—before and after breakfast. What I shouldn't be doing is looking at the Ring App on my phone and my mom's face near the camera like she's trying to see inside it.

With a low frustrated growl I get out of bed and grab a pair of sweats along with a tee. I pull on my pants then head through the house and down the stairs to the front door, slipping my shirt over my head as I go.

When I open the front door, my mom smiles like she hasn't seen me in years, and my dad rolls his eyes at her when she greets me with a chirpy, "Hey, honey, we were hoping you were home."

I look at my dad, and ask, "Seriously, you let her drag you into this?"

"Got no choice. You should know that by now. Sorry, bud." He shrugs, but he doesn't actually look sorry at all. Really, he looks like he's enjoying this.

"What's that supposed to mean?" Mom asks, looking between the two of us. "What's wrong with a mom wanting to check on her only son?"

"I don't know, Mom. Maybe the fact that I told you about Hadley, and you just couldn't control yourself long enough to meet her this evening, like I told you you would. Instead, you decided to ambush us before we've even gotten out of bed for the day."

"I'm not ambushing you," she snaps, and my dad chuckles, which makes her smack him in the stomach with the back of her hand.

"Hadley isn't even awake yet." I hope she gets my drift, but my mom is stubborn in her own ways, so she ignores me and I sigh. "Fine, just make some coffee while I wake her up and tell her what's going on."

"I can do coffee, and breakfast." She smiles happily.

"Christ." I jerk my hand through my hair. "All right, Mom, but please don't scare her off when you do finally meet her."

"I won't. I promise."

"Right." I kiss her cheek, and she smiles at my dad over her shoulder before moving into the house and up the steps. When she's halfway up, I turn to look at my dad. "Seriously?"

"What?" He smirks, and I shake my head. "It's a rite of passage."

"You're loving this."

"Yep." He pats my back then squeezes my shoulder before heading up the steps behind my mom.

I close the door and go up after them and don't stop to watch them greet Maxim, who's happy to see them both. I head straight to the bedroom and close the door. Hadley is still passed out, but without me in bed with her, she's moved to her stomach. Her hair is spread out behind her. The smooth skin of her back and the side of her breast can be seen, with the blanket barely covering her ass. I bite back a different kind of curse and take a seat on the side of the bed, sliding my fingers down her face. Her nose twitches, and then her eyes open when I call her name softly.

"Please don't tell me that you have to go to work right now," she says, finally focusing on me and the fact that I'm up.

"Nope, but my parents just showed up here, so I guess you're going to be meeting them now instead of later. Unless you want me to help you make a sheet rope and escape out the window."

The unease in her eyes slides away at my joke and a beautiful smile curves her lips. "Do those things even hold up?"

"No idea. I guess we'll find out," I say as she rolls to her back, pulling the blanket around her and tucking it under her arms.

"I'd rather not be the one to try it out. Maybe you should go first to see if it will hold," she suggests with a smile.

"You think you can hold my weight?"

She shrugs. "Probably not, but we can just tie it to the side table." She glances over at it and I do the same. My side tables are basically just a box with a small drawer; they don't even weigh twenty pounds each.

"I see you've got jokes this morning." I laugh, placing my hands on the bed on either side of her, and lean down to kiss her quickly before saying, "I'm sorry about this."

"It's not a big deal." She rests her hand on my chest. "I've already prepared myself for meeting them. I'll be okay."

"No, I'm sorry I don't get to spend all morning in bed and in you." I slide my fingers along the tops of her breasts exposed just above the blanket.

"Well then, I guess I'm sorry too." Her nose scrunches up. "There's still tomorrow, right?"

"Even if I have to tie you to the bed, toss our phones, and board up the doors and windows, we are not leaving this bed tomorrow unless it's to eat. "

"I like the way you think." She grins then puts pressure on my chest. "Now, let me up. I need to get dressed so I can meet your parents."

I don't budge; instead, I drop my face closer to her. "You sure you're okay with this?"

Her face softens and her hand comes up to rest against my jaw. "I'm sure, or as sure as I can be." She touches her mouth to mine briefly. "All of this is new for me, but I think—with talking about things—I'm becoming a little better at accepting… well, everything."

The word everything is heavy, and I pull her up against me. "Good."

"Now, let me up before your parents think we're in here…" Her cheeks turn pink as her words taper off.

"Think we're what?" I smirk, and her eyes drop to my mouth.

"You're such a jerk." She laughs, shoving against my chest and getting off the bed.

I roll to my back and then my side so I can watch her walk across the room.

"Baby, you gotta know it's adorable how shy you are when I'm not inside you."

"Honey." She stops to look at me over her shoulder. "You have to know how annoying you are whenever you open your mouth."

I don't know if it's the word honey, the small smile on her lips, or the look in her eyes. All I know is my chest tightens and the urge to kick my parents out and spend the day inside her almost overwhelms me. I get off the bed and adjust my cock, and her eyes drop to it. "Go on before my parents really do start to wonder what we're doing in here." When she licks her bottom lip I groan. "Go baby, then meet me in the kitchen when you're ready."

"Okay." She swallows hard then turns and disappears into the bathroom.

I pull in a few deep breaths, getting myself under control before I open the door to the bedroom and head for the kitchen. My mom is standing in front of the open fridge, and Dad's sitting on a stool at the island, sipping from a cup of coffee.

As soon as my mom sees me, her eyes fill with panic. "You have nothing in your fridge to make for breakfast."

"Mom—"

"Don't *Mom* me, Cobi," she cuts me off, shutting the fridge door. "What kind of man has a woman staying with him and nothing to cook for her?"

"I have a box of pancake mix in the pantry."

"Oh." She goes to the pantry and opens it up, and when she finds the box of mix, relief fills her features.

"Mom, are you nervous?"

"Of course not." She huffs. "Why in the world would I be nervous? I have nothing to be nervous about," she rambles, and Dad chuckles.

I go to where she's now dumping an excessive amount of mix into a bowl and wrap my arm around her shoulders. "It's going to be fine. Hadley is going to love you."

She looks up at me and blows out a breath. "I've never met one of your girlfriends before. Up until a couple days ago, I was wondering if you were…." I frown at her, and her eyes slide away briefly. "Well, if you were, I would have been okay with that too, just so you know."

"I'm not, but I'm glad to know you're open to that, since your daughter is."

"Really?" Her eyes search mine. "That's why she's not dating either." She looks so relieved that I almost feel bad for my lie.

"Stop fucking with your mom," Dad mutters, and I look at him to see he's chuckling. I smile right before I grunt when Mom hits me in the stomach hard.

"God, I do not know how I deal with you guys." She pulls away from me and goes back to dumping more mix in the bowl. "The two of you are just alike, and both of you do my head in."

"Mom, there are only four of us eating. I think that's plenty," I say, as she empties the entire new box into the bowl. When she slams the empty box down on the counter and looks at me, I feel my lips twitch but hold up my hand in front of me. "Ignore me. Make whatever you like."

"I will." She huffs again then her eyes go past my shoulder. Her face fills with surprise and softness.

I turn, knowing Hadley is there, then hold out my hand to her when I see she's nervously nibbling on her bottom lip. Once she places her soft, delicate hand in mine, I turn her to face my parents while I tuck her under my arm. "Mom, Dad, I'd like you to meet Hadley. Hadley, my parents, Liz and Trevor Mayson."

"Mrs. and Mr. Mayson," she says quietly. "It's nice to meet you both."

"Call me Liz," Mom says, coming forward and pulling Hadley away from me to give her a hug. "I'm so happy to meet you."

"You too," Hadley replies when Mom lets her go.

"Call me Trevor, honey." Dad gets up and comes around to kiss Hadley's cheek. When he pulls away, he looks at me and winks before going back to his coffee.

"I'm making pancakes!" Mom exclaims a little too loudly while spinning around and going to the stove.

Placing my mouth near Hadley's ear, I whisper, "Mom's a little nervous about meeting you."

"Really?" She looks up at me in surprise.

"Yeah, she's never met any of the women I've dated, so this is new for her too."

"What?" Her eyes widen. "Never?"

I shrug. "Why would I introduce them to someone, when I knew it wasn't really going anywhere?"

"Ugh." She presses her lips together, and then her nose scrunches up. When she relaxes her lips, she announces, "I think we should probably never talk about this again."

I hear my dad laugh and look at him.

"What?" He shrugs one shoulder. "I'm just enjoying my coffee."

I shake my head at him then look at Hadley. "Want some coffee?"

"Yes, please."

"Take a seat. I'll fix you a cup."

"Thanks."

I give her waist a squeeze and place my lips to her temple before I let her go.

"So, Hadley, tell me about you." Dad looks at her when she takes a seat next to him.

"Really, there's not much to tell." Her eyes go to him. "I grew up here. I went to college in Nashville, so I lived there for years and only recently moved back to town."

"I didn't know that," I say, and her eyes meet mine.

"Yeah, I rented a small apartment there. The rent was cheap and my landlord was great. I would probably still be there, but the owners put the house on the market a few months ago. When that happened, I knew it was time to move closer to my job. It's nice not having to commute every day, since that added another two hours onto my workday."

"Cobi says you're a social worker," Mom says quietly, and Hadley nods. "That's a noble profession, kind of like Cobi being a police officer."

"His job is much more important than mine." Hadley smiles at Mom then me.

"I don't think so, baby. Most of the time, I'm dealing with adults who have already chosen their path. You're helping kids direct theirs. Your job is one of the most important in the world, second to being a parent." As I finish speaking, her face is softer than I've ever seen it and her eyes are wet.

"I'll be right back," Mom says quietly before disappearing around the corner toward the half bath in the hall with her head down. Dad gets up and follows, but he gives me a look, letting me know that she'll be okay, before he goes.

"You're a good man, Cobi." My eyes leave my dad's back and meet Hadley's. "A really good man." She leans across the counter and grabs hold of my tee with a fist at my chest. When she pulls me forward, I give in to her demand and kiss her. I know she only means to touch her mouth to mine, but I deepen the kiss and touch my tongue to hers. After she drags her mouth from mine, we stare at each other until I hear my parents coming out of the bathroom. When they emerge, I can tell my mom's been crying. It's not a surprise; she's always been that way.

"Are you okay, Mrs.— I mean Liz?" Hadley asks, and Mom gives her a shaky smile.

"One thing you'll learn pretty quickly, sweetheart, is these Mayson men know how to use their words to piss you off one minute and melt your heart the next."

"I can see that." Hadley grins at my mom.

"Though, the pissing you off business happens more often than the heart melting," Mom adds.

"That so?" Dad asks, and Mom shrugs at him. "My mind must be failing me, 'cause you didn't seem pissed last night or this morning."

"Oh my," Hadley whispers.

"Trevor!" Mom snaps.

"Christ, Dad, seriously?" I growl.

"What?" Dad casually takes another sip of coffee.

"Babe, you should probably learn now that my parents do not care about PDA or anything else like that, especially my dad."

141

"Sure don't," he agrees, giving Mom a wink.

"Can we just pretend we are a normal family for one breakfast?" Mom asks.

"Sheesh, you guys are making a bad impression on Hadley," I tease.

"I'm okay, really. It's nice to get a little glimpse of why Cobi is the way he is," Hadley murmurs.

"How exactly am I?"

She tips her head to the side and answers. "Sweet, funny, affectionate, a little too honest, sometimes, okay, a lot of times, annoying."

"Just like his dad." Mom laughs and pats my chest. "Now, Hadley, how many pancakes do you want?"

"Three is good for me," she answers, and I smile at her while Mom pours batter on the griddle. When my father's eyes meet mine over the top of his cup, I know he's happy for me. I also know he understands exactly what I'm feeling right now, because it's what he's felt for my mom for years.

By the time breakfast is finished and we've said goodbye to my parents with a promise to see them later, Hadley is completely at ease with both of them. Not that I'm surprised—my parents are easy to talk to, quick to laugh, and down to earth. Unlike a lot of kids, when me and my sister were growing up, we had no issues hanging at home with our parents, and normally our friends chose to spend their time at our place instead of at their own.

Now isn't any different. If I have time off, I go to my parents' place or spend time with the rest of my family, who are exactly the same. My family is close; we have always been, and I hope with time Hadley will settle in and feel what I've felt my whole life. A connection to people, who she knows will look out for her, protect her, and have her back when she needs it most. I want that for her more than I want anything else. I want her to know deep down to her bones that she belongs, that she can be herself, and that she has a family. Because one thing I know for certain is that at the end of the day, the unconditional love a family can bring you is what will make you stronger as an individual.

Chapter 12

"SO HOW WAS IT seeing Harmony again?" Brie asks as we slide into a booth across from each other. It's the Monday after I met Cobi's parents on Saturday morning and the rest of his family that night when we went to his Uncle Nico's house for dinner. Having met Nico and Sophie at the hospital I felt at ease around them, and it didn't take me long to fall in love with the rest of Cobi's family. Just like his parents, everyone made it a point to include me and make me feel welcome. It was strange at first being around a family that actually cared and obviously loved one and other, and, if I'm honest, it made me crave that for myself. "Hadley," Brie calls, pulling me from my thoughts and bringing my attention back to the moment. "How was it?"

"Sorry," I let out a breath. "At first it was a little weird," I admit, unwrapping my fork and knife from the napkin bound around it. "Harmony and I just kind of stared at each other from across the room then she started to cry and so did I and we ran to each other."

"You cried?" Brie asks astonished.

"It was emotional," I say quietly.

"I bet. And it's understandable. You two went through something traumatic together."

I nod. "It's odd, but I feel a strange connection to her because of what happened that night."

"I think that's normal. Who knows what would have happened to her or either of you if you weren't together."

"Yeah," I agree, then look up at the waitress when she arrives. After she takes our lunch orders and leaves, I look at Brie once more. "But it was good to see for myself that she was okay and being taken care of."

"So you met all Cobi's family then?"

"Most of them, everyone who lives in the area was there." I say, placing my napkin on my lap.

"What do you think of them?" she questions, studying me.

"They're all really nice."

"Real nice or fake nice?"

"Honestly they all seem like good people, the kind of people who you'd want to have as a family. They are super close, but I never once felt uncomfortable or out of place."

"Like Cobi would ever allow you to feel uncomfortable." She rolls her eyes.

"You're right, he wouldn't. Still, I never did. Not once."

Her face is soft as she asks, "And Cobi's parents?"

"I love them," I say easily. "Even if things between Cobi and I didn't work out, I would want to keep in touch with them. His mom is sweet, and his dad is funny. I liked them instantly and love how they were together. I've never seen a couple who's been together for years still happy after all that time, but they are. Really thinking about it, his uncles and their wives are the same. They are like some kind of family science experiment that went right instead of wrong."

"I like that for you. I like the idea of you being with Cobi and having them too," she says just as the waitress arrives at the table dropping off our orders.

"I like it too." I pick up my sandwich then admit. "I'm also a little worried."

"About?"

"What if I get used to Cobi and his family and having all these great people around then things don't work out between us and..." *I'm left alone again?* I don't add.

"First, you'll always have me and Ken." She holds up one finger then adds another. "Second, if you're constantly thinking about what could go wrong, you're going to miss when things are going right. Just enjoy the moment. You told me yourself that you're taking things one day at a time with Cobi so continue to do that, continue to enjoy what you're building with him and don't let what might happen affect it."

"You're right."

"Um… when the hell have I ever been wrong?" she questions, tone faux indignant.

"Oh, I can think of a few times."

I smirk at her and she mutters, "Whatever," under her breath, making me laugh.

We dig into our food since we don't have much time before we have to get back to the office. When we're both just about finished, the waitress drops off the check and I start to dig into my bag for some cash, then stop when I hear. "You fucking bitch!" I look up and feel the color drain from my face. Mr. Shelp, Lisa and Eric's dad, is standing just inside the door of the restaurant with his angry eyes on me. "You fucking bitch!" he repeats and Brie turns to look at him briefly before swinging her head back my way.

"Do you know him?"

"He's the father of two of my kids who have recently been removed from his custody," I tell her quietly.

"Fuck!" she hisses, understanding exactly what that means as he starts to storm toward our table.

A large man wearing a construction vest blocks his path and Mr. Shelp shoves him in the chest roaring. "Get out of my way! That bitch took my fucking kids from me." He points directly at me and my pulse that was already beating hard starts to thunder as everyone in the place turns to look in my direction. Adrenalin rushes through my veins and fear fills my chest when he shoves the guy blocking him out of the way. I stand quickly and Brie does as well. When he gets to Brie, who's closer to him than me, she tries to say something to him but he puts a hand to her chest and shoves her back into the booth. I glance at her, making sure she's okay then focus on the man coming at me quickly.

"Mr. Shelp, you need to calm down and think about what you're doing right now and how this could end up affecting your case to get your children back."

"Do not fucking tell me what I should be doing." He bears down on me, shoving his finger in my face, and I smell it then, the stale whiskey, he reeks like it's coming from his pores. "You took my kids." His hand moves so fast I don't have time to prepare, and when his fingers wrap around my neck my eyes widen. I dig my nails into his arm trying to get free and stars start to fill my vision as his hold on my throat tightens. "I told you, bitch, I'd fucking hurt you!" I hear Brie shouting. I can hear commotion going on around me, but my eyes are glued to the bloodshot ones that are locked on mine as darkness starts to take over the outer edge of my vision. Suddenly the hold on my neck is gone and I collapse to the ground, my legs not strong enough to hold me up. I wrap my hands around my throat trying to breathe through the pain there. It feels almost impossible.

"Oh my God, Hadley, tell me you're okay." Brie comes into view taking my face in her hands. I try to focus on her but everything seems fuzzy like I took Nyquil but woke up before I got enough sleep. "Call an ambulance!" she screams, looking frantically behind her.

"Cops and ambulance are on the way," someone sounding far away says, just as a loud crash sounds next to me. Startled, I look to my side and see three men pinning Mr. Shelp to the ground and wrestling his arms behind his back while tables and chairs skid across the room.

"Focus on me, Hadley. Look at me, girl," Brie says and my eyes move back to her. "Are you okay?" I try to tell her that I'm good, but I can't seem to get my voice to work and end up nodding instead. "I can't believe this."

"Here take this. Put it on her neck." Someone shoves a white towel between us and Brie takes it, then gently pulls my hands from my throat where I'm holding them. When the wet cold hits my skin I flinch then sigh in relief when the cool seeps in. I hear sirens getting closer and close my eyes. I grew up learning that nothing good ever came from that sound but now I feel nothing but relief at hearing it.

"Cobi is on his way." Brie wraps her arm around my back and I rest my head on her shoulder as a different kind of relief fills me. "I seriously can't believe this happened," Brie repeats, while she takes a tight hold of my hand, keeping her other hand gently at my neck where the wet cloth is.

I don't know how, but I know the instant Cobi walks into the restaurant. His volatile energy is so strong I swear I can taste it on my tongue and feel it zipping over my skin. I open my eyes and I watch him stalk toward where I'm still sitting on the floor with Brie. When he's halfway to me his eyes move to where Mr. Shelp is still lying before they come right back to me and darken. His jaw clenches when he notices Brie's hand holding the rag to my neck and his hands ball into fists, flexing once before releasing. "Let me see, baby," he orders, dropping to his jean-covered knees at my side. Brie moves her hand away but I refuse to remove mine. I can tell he's ready to lose it and that it won't take much to send him over the edge. "Let me see, Hadley."

"You're mad," I choke out. If I thought he looked pissed before, I know I was wrong when he hears my voice and his eyes fill with rage. His hand gently tugs mine from where I'm holding the towel and his gaze scans my neck, face, and eyes.

"Why?" he asks and I don't get a chance to answer.

Brie answers for me. "He's the father of two of her kids. She recently was forced to remove them from his home."

"Christ," Cobi growls, gathering me in his arms and picking me up off the ground. He stands, holding me protectively like a child and something in my chest cracks.

"Cobi…"

"Do not talk right now," he bites out. "Gonna take you out to the ambulance. I want to make sure your windpipe is okay, and your eye." My eye? What was wrong with my eye? I don't get a chance to ask him, because he looks away from me and starts toward the door but stops suddenly and turns slightly. "Jacobs?"

"Yeah man?" a male voice returns and I look around Cobi's shoulder to see him addressing one of the cops who is now standing over Mr. Shelp's form with his boot in his back.

"You better put that motherfucker somewhere I can't get my hands on him. I swear to God, if I get a hold of him I'm going to treat him to what he treated my woman to, only I won't be pulled off or let the fuck up until I end his sorry fucking life."

"I got you, Mayson," Jacobs agrees, slapping a pair of cuffs on Shelp and then, not too gently, he and another officer jerk him up from the ground.

I look away and tuck my face into Cobi's neck when Shelp's eyes land on me and fill with hate, causing a shiver to slide down my spine. "He will not motherfucking touch you, baby. I swear to God, he will never fucking touch you." Cobi's voice rasps against my ear and tears start to slide down my cheeks. My chest aches as I fight back a sob and I twist my fingers into his shirt holding onto him as tightly as possible. When he sits down with me in his lap in the back of the ambulance, I listen to him and Brie as they talk. He tells her that she needs to let our boss know what happened, and that I won't be in the office today. I don't even try to argue with him and tell him that I have to work. I don't think I could if I wanted to and I don't. Everything I have been keeping locked away inside me is bubbling to the surface and tears I can't control are running down my face in what feels like rivers. My body bucks on a quiet sob and Cobi holds me closer, telling me with his lips to my ear to let it all go. I bury my face against his chest and cry. I cry through the paramedics checking me over, cry while Cobi places me in his truck, and continue to cry when he tucks me into his bed before I eventually cry myself to sleep.

I awaken in the dark and lie there on my back, looking up at the ceiling and the light from the open blinds dancing across it. I can hear voices just outside the door talking quietly, and I know three of them are Kenyon, Brie, and Cobi. The others I can't place. My eyes burn because I've cried so much and my throat's sore and dry. With a pounding at the back of my skull that will only be cured with Tylenol, I toss back the blankets covering me and sit up. Carefully, I get out of bed and go to the bathroom. I search until I find something to take for my headache, splash water on my face, and then lean closer to the mirror, when my eye catches my attention. The white is blood red, probably from the pressure

Mr. Shelp exerted when he was choking me. My eyes drop to my neck where a purple and ugly shade of green collar circles my throat. My head falls forward and I bring my hands toward my face, fingers curled into my palms. When I see the dried blood under my nails, my chest burns. I flip the hot water on, grab the hand soap, and start to scrub my hands together. My throat works as I try to swallow down a new wave of tears. When the blood doesn't wash away, I whimper in distress, add more soap, and scrub harder. I hold my hands under the hot water and bend forward, resting my forehead to the cold counter, needing to calm down so I can breathe.

The water goes off and a strong arm wraps around me from behind. "I got you, baby," Cobi says gently.

I shake my head frantically back and forth. "I can't get his blood out from under my nails."

"Let me see." Grabbing my hips he moves me around to face him, then lifts me up to sit on the counter. I watch him take my hands between his and lift them to his lips. "There's nothing there, baby. You got them all clean."

"Why did he do that?" I drop my forehead to his chest with my hands still captured between us. "Why couldn't he just do the right thing and clean himself up for his kids?" I draw in a shaky breath, trying to allow the feeling of him close relax me.

"You'll never get those answers, babe. I think you know that better than most people do." *God, do I ever...* At the same time I don't at all, because I cannot imagine having a child, or children, taken from me because of my own stupidity then refusing to do everything within my power to get them back.

"Is he still in jail?" Panic fills me at the idea of him being out. I know the officers were taking him in when I was still crying on Cobi's lap, but I don't know if he was released on bail, because I've been asleep since Cobi brought me back to his place.

Releasing the hold he has on me, he slides his hands up between us then around each side of my neck tipping my face back toward him. His eyes move over me and his anger from earlier comes back as they land on my neck and the bruising there.

"He won't see a judge until morning, and no way will I allow him to get off easy. He assaulted you in a public place with witnesses. Each and every person there agreed that if they hadn't intervened he would have killed you."

"Cobi," I whisper, not sure what I can say to defuse the situation.

"I'm going to personally make sure he serves time, and a lot of it, for what he did and his reasoning for doing it."

"Okay," I agree, resting my palms against his chest where I can feel his heart pounding hard.

He drops his forehead to mine and keeps his gaze on mine as he speaks, "Life is not always roses. And I understand better than most that sometimes people slip up and make mistakes but I know—" His fingers on my neck slide ever so lightly across my skin. "—I know that if you want something better, you'll get up, dust yourself off, find a way to right your wrongs, and make that happen." His steady voice drops to a growl as he continues, "What you won't do is blame someone else for up your fuck up and then take your pain out on them. He had no right to be pissed at you, no right to get in your space, and no fucking right to put his hands on you the way he did."

"You're right," I state gently, hoping to calm him.

"I want to kill him." His eyes close like he's in pain.

I move my hands up his chest. Hoping to soothe him in some way, I run the tips of my fingers over his jaw saying quietly, "I'm okay."

"I know, but swear to Christ when I saw you and the bruises around your neck I knew if I didn't focus on taking care of you, I'd put my hands on him and end his life."

"I'm glad you didn't do that," I whisper.

"I wouldn't regret it if I did, Hadley." He focuses his eyes on mine, and his jaw clenches before he starts to speak again. "That's the kind of guy you are falling in love with, the kind of guy who wouldn't care about his future if something happened to you. Are you okay with that?"

"I would be really mad at you if you ever did something so stupid because you'd be taken from me, but you don't scare me, Cobi Mayson. I like that you're protective of the people you care about, even those that you don't know. I like the way you make me feel safe when I'm with you and taken care of even when we aren't together." I pull in a breath after I finish, then wonder if he's actually trying to warn me off and do it gently. If he's trying to find a way to get me to be the one to end things so he doesn't have to.

"Hadley…"

Normally I would never have the courage to ask, but with my heart on the line I don't even hesitate. "Are you trying to scare me off so I'll walk away from you?"

"What?" His head jerks back and he frowns. "How does that question even make sense after what I just said to you?"

"I don't know." I toss my hands out. "You're being intense and scary. I just don't know if you're doing it to scare me off or to warn me of what the future might look like if we keep going forward."

"I'm letting you know the kind of man I am, Hadley," he says with a frustrated grunt.

"Okay then, I get it. You're overprotective and possibly crazy. Can we be done talking about this now? I'm kind of hungry. I also think I heard you talking to Brie and Kenyon. If they're here then they're probably worried and I need to make sure they know I'm okay."

"Seriously?" he asks in disbelief.

"What? Did you want to tell me more about what a caveman you are?" I deepen my voice. "Me go look for food, you stay here and sweep cave, pop out babies and cook."

"What the fuck have I gotten myself into with you?" he asks, tipping his head back toward the ceiling.

I grin, then lose hold on my smile and rest my hands against him. "I'm good, you're good, and I'm not sure I could stop falling in love with you if I tried. I'm over my freak-out for now, though I do reserve the right to have another. But right now I'm okay. Okay?"

"Yeah, baby." He brushes his mouth over mine and leans back smiling.

"Though I think you might be the crazy one between us, just so you know." He might be right thinking about all the emotions I've gone through the last few hours I feel like I might be crazy.

"It's a possibility," I agree while he pulls me from the counter. "You

153

might want to run for the hills while you still have the chance."

"I like crazy." He pulls me against his chest and wraps his arms around me, keeping his head dipped toward mine. "A lot." His mouth touches mine in a soft sweet kiss.

I open my eyes when he pulls his mouth away and ask, "Who's here?"

"My parents, Brie, and her man." He takes my hand to lead me from the bathroom then stops before opening the door to the bedroom and looks down at me. "My family all wanted to come but mom told them to give you a couple days. They're worried about you." I melt against him. "You have a lot of people who care about you, baby." He wraps his hand around the side of my neck and smooths his thumb along my jaw.

"Because of you."

"No, because of you. Because of the person you are."

"Don't make me cry again. I think I've reached my quota for the day," I tell him, not really joking.

"I don't want you to cry. I just want you to know that you're worth worrying about, worth caring about. That you deserve to have good people in your life because you're a good person."

"I'm starting to believe that," I say quietly, and I am. I don't know if it's talking with my doctor, or what Brie has been telling me forever, or if it's Cobi beating down my defenses, but I'm starting to believe that I'm someone worth knowing. Someone worthy of a guy like him. A good man who sees something in me I don't always see in myself.

"Now come on so I can feed you and you can reassure the people who care about you that you're okay." He doesn't give me a chance to respond before he touches his mouth to mine and leads me from the bedroom, out to his family and mine, to the people who I know really care about me.

Hadley

Cobi

Cobi

Chapter 13

"SO HOW'S EVERYTHING GOING with Hadley?" my partner Frank asks, studying me.

We stopped at Banks, the bar next to the station, after we both got off duty. Me, because I needed to kill time before going home, since Hadley is at her doctor's appointment. Frank, because his wife and three daughters are home—in his words—driving him up the wall about putting in a pool while the costs are down this winter. Having met his wife, Stacey, and his girls, ranging from ages twelve to seventeen, I can see this. Though, I know Frank and know he's gonna give in to them; he just needs to do it in his own time.

I take a drag from my beer while I pull my elbows from the table and lean back against the chair. "She's healing. The bruising is just about gone. But she's still worried about Shelp."

"He's in jail. She knows he can't hurt her again, right?" he asks, concern filling his voice.

"It's not about that. She's never liked the part of her job that involves splitting up families, and she knows with what he did he's going away for a while. She doesn't like that she's the catalyst for that."

"It's his own damn fault for not pulling his head out of his ass,"

Frank grumbles.

"You're not telling me anything I don't know. It's just her; she's soft, thinks that most people, given the time and chance, will do the right thing." How she's not jaded after the way she grew up is anyone's guess, but she's not. She really believes everyone is good or has good in them.

"It's good with her job she thinks like that, but sometimes people just don't give a fuck about anyone but themselves."

"You're not wrong." I glance at my cell when the screen lights up with a text from her, letting me know she's out of her appointment and heading to her car. After I read it, I look at Frank.

"Go on. I'm gonna drink another before I head home to chaos and more talk about the pool." He lifts his beer.

"Just give in and the conversation will end." I grin at him.

"Kid, you think it works like that, you're in for a rude awakening in about five years. If it's not one thing, it's another, and sometimes you gotta put your foot down to prove a point."

"Well, old-timer, you've been married to Stacey for what, twenty-three years? I say stick to what's working for you." He grins, and with that I stand, tossing some cash on the table. "See you tomorrow."

"Yeah, tell Hadley I said hi."

"Will do." I give him a chin lift and head for my truck.

I stop on the way home and pick up a pizza with everything from Marco's then drive to my place. I don't see Hadley's car until I hit the remote for the garage, which means I'm smiling as I pull into one of the lot spaces. I told her for three days I wanted her car inside my single-car garage. For three days, she ignored me and parked in the lot, telling me it didn't make sense, since she normally left before me in the morning.

After I shut down the engine, I get out, taking the pizza with me through the garage. I hit the button to close the door then head up the stairs. Maxim doesn't greet me at the door, and I know why when I see Hadley at the island, head tipped down with a glass of wine in front of her. Seeing her posture, I know she parked in the garage not thinking about what she was doing; her mind was on other shit.

Fuck.

I should have met her at her appointment, done a quick pulse check, and then decided if she was good to drive, especially after what just went down and what talking about it could bring up for her.

"Baby." Her head comes up and her blank eyes meet mine, freaking me right the fuck out. "What's going on?"

"My mom's in the hospital." At her statement, I pause and she lifts her glass of wine to her lips.

"Say that again?" I walk to the counter and set down the pizza.

"My dad had been calling me. I was fed up, didn't want to deal with him, so I blocked his number from my phone. He tracked me down tonight when I got out of my appointment. He caught me at my car after I sent you the text to let you know I was heading home."

"He told you your mom's in the hospital?" I ask, getting close to her. "Yes."

"What's wrong with her?"

She chews the inside of her cheek before answering. "He said he thinks she got ahold of Fentanyl pills. When he found her in her bed, she was barely breathing, her lips and nails were blue, and it was obvious she'd overdosed." She takes a breath as I wrap her in my arms. "He couldn't get her to wake up, so he called an ambulance. She's been in the hospital for three days and hasn't improved. The doctors told him that they don't think she'll make it much longer and that everyone needs to know so they can say goodbye."

My eyes close as I rest my chin on top of her head. "I'm sorry, baby."

"Me too," she whispers.

"Do you want me to take you tonight?" I question, leaning back to look at her, but her eyes are pointed at my throat.

"No." She shakes her head then glances up at me, looking conflicted. "But I know I need to go."

"Then we'll go." I kiss the top of her head then release her. I help her into her coat then lead her to my truck and help her inside. She's silent on the way to the hospital, but the moment I reach out and take hold of her hand, her fingers close tightly around mine.

I park near the entrance and lead her to the nurses' station, letting them know who we're looking for and getting a room number. When we make it to the door to her mom's room, I stop her outside and turn her toward me. Getting her attention, I slide one hand around her back, the other around the nape of her neck.

"Cobi," she starts, but I cut her off, tightening my hands where they're wrapped around her.

"Whatever happens, you are not alone, baby. Remember that when we walk through those doors and back out of them when it's over." Her eyes warm and she nods. "I'm here for whatever you need."

"Thank you." Her bottom lip trembles, and my stomach muscles constrict at the sight. It kills me to see her in pain.

"It's gonna be okay."

"Okay," she agrees softly.

I kiss her then let her go, taking her hand as she reaches for me. When we walk into the room, it's empty except for the bed where her mother is lying on her back, the covers up to her shoulders. Her hair is almost the color of Hadley's, with silver mixed in. It's on top of her head in a bun, and her skin is so pale it looks almost blue. Even from the door, I can hear a rattle in her chest every time she takes a breath—a sound I know means she's just like the doctors said, probably not going to last much longer.

I let Hadley set the pace and lead me to the bed, her steps slow, and I can feel her hand shaking. When we stop near her mom's head, I slide my arm around her waist when she lets my hand go to reach out and touch the side of her mom's face.

"I wish things had been different," she says quietly, her words filled with pain, longing, sadness, and defeat. "I wish…." Before she can finish, she sobs and turns toward me, burying her face in my chest and wrapping her arms around me, clinging to me like a child who's lost.

I don't hesitate for a moment. I pick her up and carry her out of the room and the hospital, ignoring the looks from people as we pass. When we hit my truck, it takes some maneuvering to keep her in my arms and get the door open, but I get her inside and buckled up before I head around the back and get in behind the wheel.

When we're back at my place, I carry her to bed and get her undressed and changed. Through it all, she silently cries, and then she cries some more as I curl myself around her and hold her until she falls asleep.

Once I know she's resting, I get up, take Maxim out, and make a few calls. A friend of my family, Justin, is my first call, and he gets me the number for her dad.

When the man answers, I can tell he's drunk, and that pisses me off. I don't get into that with him; I let him know that when his wife passes, he needs to contact me so I can tell his daughter. He agrees and I hang up. After that, I call Brie then my mom and my cousins, who have all been in constant contact with Hadley the last few days. When her mom does pass, regardless of their relationship, she's going to need people around her who care.

After I hang up on the last call, I go get back into bed with her. The moment I do, she turns to me and fits herself against my side in her sleep. I hold her close and stay awake through the night so that if she wakes up I'm there to make sure she's okay. She doesn't wake up, not until my phone on the nightstand rings with a call from her dad, letting me know the hospital called to tell him that Charlene passed away.

Chapter 14

SITTING ON LIZ AND Trevor's very comfortable couch in their beautiful house, I scan the living room and kitchen, taking each person in. The space is crowded with Cobi's entire family—aunts and uncles, cousins I met before today, and others I met just a few hours ago, along with some of their significant others—Brie, and Kenyon. Everyone is standing or sitting while chatting, eating, and drinking. All of them gathered together because of me.

My eyes catch on Harmony's, and she gives me a sad but reassuring smile. I give her a small smile in return then look down at my lap, pulling in a breath. Today was my mother's funeral. Not an actual funeral—my dad couldn't afford to have one for her, and I could only help out so much with the cost of what we did have. The service was small; a few people from the bar my mom worked at showed up, along with Dad, some of his friends, then me, and this room full of people made up the rest.

Cobi's parents' pastor came to say a few words at the gravesite before my mother's cheap casket was lowered into the ground, and his aunts all brought flowers to be tossed in on top before the earth was settled over her. It was nice, much nicer than my mom probably deserved.

At that thought, my throat gets tight, but not for the reasons it should. It's tight, because over the last few days, I've had to accept that my mom's and my relationship will never be more than what it was when she was alive. I didn't really like her much. I never felt a bond or a connection to her. She was just my mom, the woman who gave birth to me, nothing more, and that's a hard pill to swallow, especially after spending so much time with Cobi's family.

It's difficult at times to watch them interact, to see them tease each other and be affectionate. They all genuinely care about one another's well-being and happiness. They are the definition of family—*real* family. Something I never experienced before.

When weight settles into my side, I lift my head and look at Brie.

"You okay?" she asks, studying me.

"Yeah."

"Liar." She grins, bumping her shoulder into mine. Then her expression turns serious. "I wish I knew what to say to make this easier for you, but I know there are no words to make it better." She takes one of my hands, locking our fingers together. "But it will get easier. The more time that passes, the less pain you'll feel every day."

I know she's speaking from experience. I know that's how it is for her after losing both her parents. But our stories aren't even close to the same.

"We weren't even a little close. To me, she was just someone I knew, who happened to be my mom. I'm just trying to come to terms with that," I admit, feeling somewhat guilty for not being devastated by the loss of my own mother.

"Hadley, I know you and know you believed somewhere deep down that maybe she'd change one day. And now it sucks, because you'll never get that answer. That's the pain you're going to have to work through," she says firmly but quietly.

"It's scary how well you know me."

"We've been besties forever. I know you better than you know yourself." She squeezes my fingers.

I crush hers in return, muttering, "True."

"On the bright side, you've got a lot of people who are here for you while you work through that, so you're not alone."

I look away from her and glance around the room again. My eyes land on Cobi, who's chatting with his cousin July's husband, a guy named Wes, who I met this afternoon. Both men are laughing about whatever they are talking about. Feeling my eyes on him, Cobi looks at me and his face softens. At that look, my heart flips and my stomach bottoms out.

I have no doubt I'm in love with him. He's taken care of me since the moment we met, reassured me when I've had doubts, and pushed through every one of my defenses. I've never met a man like him before, and I know that's because men like him only exist in romance novels, fairy tales, and Disney movies. But somehow, he's living and breathing.

"If you're still questioning if you're in love with that man, I swear I'll kick your ass," Brie cuts into my thoughts, and I pull my eyes from Cobi's to look at her.

"As if you could."

She could. She's taller than me by at least four inches, has a little more weight than I do—all distributed in just the right places—and she's avid about working out. Something I'm allergic to doing.

"I so totally could. I just wouldn't, because I don't feel like chipping a nail or messing up my hair," she says, and I laugh. Brie has always been about her appearance. She's beautiful, with dark skin, long almost black hair that ends past her shoulders, almond-shaped eyes, high cheekbones, and full lips. She never misses an appointment to get her hair done each month, and goes to the nail salon once more besides the time we go together.

"Keep telling yourself that, babe," I say.

She smiles then rests her head on my shoulder. "I love you."

I close my eyes and let those words seep in. As a constant in my life, I've always known I cared about Brie, but now I know that when she's said I love you and I've said it back, I *did* actually mean it. Until recently, I wasn't exactly sure what love was. I didn't really understand that love is more than just a word people say to those they care about. Love is being there for someone when they need you the most. It's worrying about someone else's happiness and wanting that for them more than you want it for yourself. It's showing up and fighting through the hard stuff, because you know it will be worth it in the end.

"I love you too," I finally get out. "Thank you for always being here for me when I've needed you."

"Always, Hadley, you have my word that you will always have me."

I don't reply; I can't without crying, and I don't want to cry. Instead, I tighten my hold on her fingers then tip my head to the side to kiss the top of her head. I hear her pull in a breath and pull in one of my own. When I open my eyes back up, I catch Kenyon sharing a look with Brie with a small smile on his lips before he goes back to talking to Harmony's dad, Nico.

"Cobi's family's cool. I want them to adopt me," Brie says, lifting her head off my shoulder.

"Right?"

"Though I don't think it's normal to think your family is hot, so maybe I won't." I burst out laughing, tossing my head back, and Brie laughs along with me before getting up, still smiling. "I'm going to get another plate of food. Do you want anything?"

"No, I'm good." I grab the glass of wine I set down earlier and take a sip.

"Be back." She heads toward the kitchen, and a second later, a large shadow looms over me.

When I look up and see Harlen, I brace myself because of the look on his face. He takes a seat where Brie was but keeps his elbows to his knees, turning only his head in my direction.

"I never got a chance to thank you for what you did," he says, looking into my eyes, and my chest gets tight. "Thank you."

"I…. You're welcome. But I'm not sure I did anything," I say quietly.

"She would have been alone. She would have gone through that alone if you hadn't been there with her. So yeah, you did something," he replies, his jaw getting hard.

"Okay."

"Anything you need, I got your back."

I take him in. He's very good-looking, but also very scary—definitely someone people would walk the other way from in a dark alley. Still, I knew from seeing him with Harmony that he's also soft and sweet. Well, at least with her he is.

"I'll keep that in mind if I ever need some muscle," I joke to ease the tension I feel coming off of him, and he grins.

"You got it if you need it." He stands then reaches out, touching the top of my head before going across the room directly to Harmony. When he's close, he slides his arm around her waist and kisses the side of her head. I see her face get soft and know the reason for it, because I've felt that exact thing when Cobi has done that to me.

I finish off the last of my wine and get up off the couch, going to the kitchen. When I get there, I see Liz starting to put things away and his aunts washing dishes. I begin to help clear one of the counters of food, but stop when a hand gently smooths down the back of my head and lips touch my cheek. I look at Liz standing at my side, and she gives me a small smile. "You doin' okay, honey?"

She's asked me that question a lot the last few days. She's called just to ask me if I'm all right, and sent texts asking the same. It feels good that she cares so much, and I honestly don't know what I would have done without her, Cobi, and Trevor, who have all held my hand every step of the way.

"I'm okay," I reassure her.

"You don't need to help with this. We've got it under control," she says, and I look at Cobi's aunts, who I can tell have done this before.

"I don't mind."

"I know you don't, but I do. You need to relax. Really, you should probably have Cobi take you home so you can get some rest. It's been a long day for you."

"I—"

"Sweetheart, just give in," Sophie says, coming toward us and cutting me off. "She's not going to let up. Plus, she isn't wrong. It's been a long day, so you should go home, take a bath, and relax."

"Mom's not wrong, and neither is Aunt Sophie," Cobi states, coming into the kitchen, wrapping his arms around me from behind, and resting his chin on my shoulder. "I was just coming to find you to tell you it's time to head out."

"I want to help clean up." I turn my head to look at him.

"Like Liz and Sophie said, we've got it, honey," his aunt November says, while his aunt Lilly nods in agreement. "Go on home and rest."

"I—"

"Please," Liz murmurs, resting her hand on the side of my face. "I know you want to help, but you can do that by letting us take care of you."

"Oh, all right." I sigh, and Cobi chuckles, moving from behind me and taking my hand.

"Say goodnight, baby."

"You're really annoying when you're bossy," I tell him, and his mom and aunts all laugh while he just kisses the side of my head. Before we go, I say goodnight to everyone, including Brie and Kenyon, and then Cobi takes me out to his truck and settles me inside.

When we arrive at the townhouse and get upstairs, he pours me a glass of wine, leaving it on the kitchen counter before disappearing in the bedroom. Just as I'm hooking Maxim's leash to his collar, Cobi comes out of the bedroom. I watch him go to the kitchen and grab my glass of wine then come toward me holding it. He takes Maxim's leash from me and hands me the glass.

"Bath's running. Go on and get in. I'll be back soon."

"Wait… What?" I blink at the glass now in my hand then him.

"Bath, baby." He gently shoves me toward the bedroom. I walk toward the bedroom, but pause to watch him. "Go, baby," he orders, looking at me before closing the door. After a deep breath, I go through the bedroom and into the bathroom, and stop at the door.

The lights are dim and the large freestanding bathtub is filling with steaming water and fluffy bubbles. I set my glass of wine on the edge of the tub then take off my coat. I hang it in the closet then strip out of my heels and the simple black dress I wore today. I tie my hair up on top of my head and get into the tub, sighing when the hot water touches my skin.

Once I'm sitting in the water, I look around the bathroom. Like the rest of the house, it's beautiful. There's a glass-enclosed shower with cream, jade, and white glass tiles in the corner of the room. The walls are painted cream, and the floor matches the rest of the house, which is rustic wood. There's a long vanity and double sinks, each with a mirror above, and fluffy rugs and towels.

I pick up my glass of wine, trying to remember if I have ever taken a bath before. I probably did when I was little, but I don't remember. The trailer I grew up in had a bathtub, but it was small, and I wouldn't take a bath there unless I had a tetanus shot beforehand. There was more rust than paint on the inner surface, and some sharp spots that would cut you if you weren't careful. I set my glass down and lean back, closing my eyes and allowing the sound of the running water and heat to relax me.

A finger gently slides between my eyes and down to the tip of my nose, and I open my eyes. "Hey, baby," Cobi says, resting his elbows on the edge, his shirtsleeves now rolled up his forearms.

"I fell asleep," I tell him, something he obviously knows, and he smiles, touching his finger to my cheek.

His eyes move over the parts of me not covered with bubbles before coming back to mine. "How's the water?"

"Nice, warm." I take his hand and study his tattooed skin against mine. "I can't remember ever taking a bath."

"Do you like it?"

"Yes..." I look into his beautiful eyes. "But I'd like it more if you were in here with me."

"I can do that," he replies, standing. I watch him pull his shirt from his slacks then unbutton it, exposing his wide chest and abs. He slips it off his shoulders, tossing it toward the closet, and then he unhooks his belt before it flies to the closet too. When he removes his pants and boxers and I see he's hard, my nipples pebble and my core tightens. He shuts off the water and gets in opposite me, his knees bent with his legs on the outside of mine. "Better?" he asks, and I shake my head. "What do you need, baby?"

"You, always you," I whisper, and he takes my hand and pulls me across the water to him until his slick body is under mine and his erection is resting against my lower belly. His hands wrap around my hips, and I slide my hips up. I feel him nudge my entrance with the tip of his cock, and I take his face in my hands. I touch my mouth to his before leaning back to look into his eyes. "I love you." At my admission, his body tightens and his hold, already firm, grows possessive. "I know it's probably too soon, but I want you to know."

"Hadley—"

"I…." I cut him off then shake my head. "You're the best man I have ever met in my life, the best thing to ever happen to me."

"I love you too," he growls, thrusting up into me but locking me there with his hands, his eyes still on mine. "You belong to me, don't you?"

"Yes," I breathe, dropping my forehead to his. "Always."

"Until the end, until one of us ceases to exist, we belong to each other."

Tears fill my eyes and I rest my mouth on his. "Until the end." It's a vow, a promise to him and to myself.

"I want you to move in with me," he says as he starts to rock me on his length.

I start to open my mouth to tell him it's too soon for that, but gasp when he drags his hips back then thrusts up into me hard, causing water to splash out of the tub onto the floor.

"You just told me you belong to me. I'm not putting it off. I want you here with me. Want to take care of you."

His words hit me directly in the heart and I agree with a whimpered, "Okay," as he thrusts into me again.

"Tomorrow," he growls, and I start to laugh. "What's funny?" He stops moving.

I slide my fingers into his hair and lean over him. "I…" I roll my hips into his and he grunts. "I'm screwed. I can't seem to ever say no to you."

"You're definitely screwed." He tips his head down and captures my breast, pulling my nipple into his mouth. Sucking hard, he lifts his hips on each of my downward strokes. Water sloshes over the side of the tub as we move together in sync. He takes hold of my neglected breast and squeezes, then slides his hand to between my legs, rolling my clit, as my head falls back to my shoulders.

"Cobi," I breathe as my eyes slide closed.

"Look at me, baby." My head tilts forward and my eyes lock with his. "I love you."

"I know," I whimper, holding his gaze.

His finger circles harder and my hands move to his shoulders to hold on. As my nails dig into his flesh, he leans up and captures my mouth. I open for him, hoping to pour into that kiss everything I feel for him, hoping that he fully understands what he means to me. As I start to clamp down and spasm around him, he groans into my mouth while his hips jerk. I come, feeling him become impossibly bigger as he releases deep inside me. Panting for breath and seeing stars, my body falls limply against his. His arms slide around my back and he tucks his face into my neck, breathing heavy, his heart pounding between us, my heart beating just as hard. We both cling to each other until the water starts to get cool.

"Gotta get up, baby," he tells me, and I lean back slightly to look at him, every one of my muscles protesting against me. When he pulls his hips from mine, a soft mewl escapes and my eyes close. "I got you." He somehow has the strength I don't to lift me into his arms and step out of the tub.

When he sets me down and water sloshes under my feet, I look down then up at him. "Oops."

"Don't worry about that right now." He lets me go with a smile then wraps me in a towel and picks me back up. He carries me to the bed, where he deposits me before tossing the covers over me. I roll to my side, and he leans down, searching my eyes before gently placing a soft kiss to my lips. "Be back."

He stands, and I watch him go to the bathroom. When he comes back out a few minutes later, he's still naked, and his cock is still somewhat hard. I take him in, wondering what I did to deserve him. It's not his looks—those are just a bonus. Even if he were a hundred pounds overweight and balding, I would still feel thankful that I could call him mine.

He pulls back the blanket, and I cry out as he rips the towel from my body and tosses it behind him to the floor. He turns on the lamp then goes back to shut off the light before he gets into bed with me, dragging me against his side. I curl up against him with my ear over his heart, thinking about everything that has happened in such a short time.

"You're quiet," he states, running his fingers down my arm lying over his stomach.

"I'm trying to come to terms with things," I say, lifting my head and resting my chin on his pec.

"What?"

"Well…" I feel my lips twitch. "Apparently, you're in love with me, and I'm moving in with you. It's a lot to accept and I'm working through it silently."

"I see." He leans up to place his lips to my forehead before he rests his head back on his pillow.

"And, um… now that we're not in the heat of the moment, I should tell you. My lease is for a year and I've only been in the house a few months, so we're going to wait for me to move in."

"I'll talk to your landlord," he says easily, and I feel my body get tight.

"Tom."

"Excuse me?"

"Tom is my landlord. You met him briefly when he came to tell me I could get a dog," I remind him, and recognition fills his eyes. "That said, I don't think it would be a good idea for you to try to get me out of my lease."

"Why not?" He frowns.

"I'm pretty sure Tom is in the Witness Protection Program, because he was in the mob or is still in the mob." I grimace. "Can you get out of the mob, or is it like a blood in, blood out type of thing?"

"Blood in, blood out?" he repeats, looking at me like I might be crazy.

"That doesn't matter." I shake my head. "The point is I think he might be in Witness Protection now, and he's scary. It would suck if you suddenly went missing."

"You do know you're crazy, right?" he asks, but I know by the way he says it he also thinks I'm being cute.

"How am I crazy?"

"Your landlord is not in the mob, and he's not in Witness Protection either."

"How do you know?"

"I just do. Now, as for you getting out of your lease, I'll talk to him and see what he says. You might have to keep the lease for a couple of months until he can find a new renter, but we can get the ball moving now, and you can still move in here in the meantime."

I move and rest my chin on the back of my hand against his chest. "Not that I don't think this will work, but I think it's a good idea I keep my place for a few months just in case."

"It's going to work, Hadley." He slides his fingers into my hair, wrapping them around the back of my skull. "I promise you, this is going to work."

"I believe you." I kiss his chest then rest my head back down. After closing my eyes, I order, "Go to sleep," and giggle when his body shakes with silent laughter.

"'Night, baby." He rolls so we're chest-to-chest with my face resting in the crook of his neck and his arms tight around me.

And like always when I fall asleep with him, I do it smiling.

Chapter 15

"SHE SEEMS DIFFERENT."

At Kenyon's comment, I look at where he's lounging on my deck with a beer in his hand. He and Brie came over for dinner tonight, and after we ate, the girls kicked us out so they could clean up and talk about wedding stuff. I didn't put up a fight, and neither did Kenyon. We left them to it and came outside with our beers.

"She seems lighter, even with everything that's happened."

He's not wrong. She's changed the last few weeks. She's opening up a little more every day and getting more and more comfortable with me, and with us. I thought I got all of her; I thought I understood the woman she was. But I had no clue just how sweet and funny she really is. She's perfect... perfect for me.

"She's happy. Not the fake happy she used to be, just plain happy. Thank you for giving that to her," he finishes.

"I would say you're welcome, but since I'm the one benefiting from it, I think you'll get why I don't."

He grins at me then sobers. "Has her dad been in contact since—"

"No," I cut him off, knowing his question.

"Dick," he hisses, shaking his head. "Not even a call to say thank you for paying for her mom's funeral?"

"Not even for that." I take a pull from my beer to cool down the anger that's suddenly burning my throat. When the funeral home that her mom's body was sent to called, saying they were given her number by her father to settle the bill, I almost lost my shit. I couldn't believe him, but Hadley was not the least bit surprised. That also pissed me off. It told me just how used to picking up the slack and taking care of things she was.

In the end, there was nothing she could do. She couldn't leave her mom where she was. She didn't have a choice; she had to take care of things and flat out refused for me to help her in any way.

"I gotta say, as much as it pisses me off, I'm glad he's staying away. She doesn't need him fucking with her progress or her life."

"You're not wrong about that." I lift my beer toward him, and he does the same in return.

When the sliding glass door opens, I turn to watch Hadley step out, followed by Brie, both women carrying a glass of wine.

"What are you two talking about?" Hadley asks while she sits sideways on my lap instead of taking the chair next to mine.

I wrap an arm around her waist and kiss her neck, saying there, "Just guy shit."

Brie takes up the same position in Kenyon's lap with a soft smile on her face directed our way.

"Did you get the wedding stuff sorted?" Kenyon asks, and she looks down at him.

"For now," she retorts, and his eyes come to me.

"Advice, man. Do yourself a favor and elope."

I chuckle, and Hadley giggles.

"Seriously?" Brie snaps, glaring at him.

"Baby—" His voice softens. "—I love you. I wanna be your husband, but I do not want to hear about wedding shit day and night. And I have been listening to you talk about wedding shit day and night for months. And I'll remind you we still have months to go, so I don't see that changing anytime soon."

"I don't talk about wedding stuff day and night," she argues, glaring.

"So who's excited for Halloween?" Hadley asks suddenly, and everyone looks at her. "I'm thinking this year I'm going to dress up Maxim as a dragon and go as Khaleesi. How cute would that be?"

"Nice save, babe." Brie rolls her eyes, and Kenyon and I both laugh.

"On that note, we should get going." Kenyon stands, taking Brie with him and putting her on her feet.

"We have to leave already?" Brie pouts, looking up at him.

"I gotta open the shop in the morning, so I can afford to pay for our wedding," he says gently.

She tips her head to the side, her face soft. "I promise it will be worth it."

"Having you as my wife will be worth it," he murmurs, and her eyes twinkle while Hadley melts into me. "Having you happy is a bonus." He kisses her forehead then wraps an arm around her shoulders. He moves them around the table and pats my arm. "See you around, man, and thanks for dinner and the beer."

"Anytime," I say as he then leans down to kiss Hadley's cheek. "Love you."

"Love you too." She smiles at him then she gets up to give Brie a hug. I follow her up and kiss Brie's cheek then, hand in hand, Hadley and I walk them to the door.

When they're gone, I look down at her. "So you're going to dress Maxim up as a dragon?"

She laughs, tossing her head back, and I soak in the sound and look of happiness on her face.

"I didn't want them to argue." She shrugs, going toward the kitchen. "And believe me, if I didn't cut in, that would have been an argument." Her expression softens. "Kenyon didn't lie; he just wants Brie to be his wife. He doesn't care about any of the other stuff, but Brie wants a big wedding. She's always wanted a big wedding, and talked about it before Kenyon was even in the picture."

"How big is the wedding going to be?" I ask, leaning back against the counter and watching her put a few stray dishes in the dishwasher.

"Huge, over two hundred people are coming and everything is totally over the top. I'm talking crystals and floral centerpieces that you'd see in a movie huge."

"Now I see why he suggested we elope."

"Yep," she agrees, grinning at me.

"So do you want a wedding like that?" I ask, studying her.

"Me?" She shakes her head. "I don't even know a hundred people, and I haven't really ever thought about getting married, let alone having a wedding."

"My mom will want us to do something big." My mom will; that's just her, and my aunts and grandmothers are the same way. They don't need much of a reason to plan a party.

"What?" She frowns at me, shutting the door on the dishwasher.

"When we get married, my mom will want us to do something big. Maybe not two hundred people big, but she will want us to have a wedding, and she'll want to help plan it."

"I'd like to point out that you're talking about a wedding like it's going to happen."

"'Cause it is. Not right now, but it will happen. It's inevitable." I shrug.

"Moving in, marriage, next thing I know, you're going to be talking about having babies," she says softly, and I close the distance between us and wrap my hand around her hip while placing my other on the nape of her neck.

"I want three, and at least one girl," I state, and her pupils enlarge.

"Cobi." My name comes out rough while her hands spasm at my sides where they came to rest.

"Do I make you happy?" I ask with my face close to hers.

"Yes." Her eyes search mine while her hands move to my chest.

"Do you want to spend the rest of your life with me?"

"Yes." Her fingertips dig into my skin through my shirt.

"Do you want kids?"

"I… well…." Her eyes search mine again and close briefly. "With you, yes."

"We'll start tomorrow," I say, keeping my face straight, and her eyes widen. "I'm kidding, babe."

"You're such a jerk." She pushes at my chest, and I laugh, gathering her against me and shoving my face in her neck. "I can't believe you." She giggles, and I lean away, catching her eye.

"You love it."

"Kinda." Her expression softens. "Maybe it's me who's insane then."

"Probably." I smirk, and she shoves my chest again, but I don't let her go. Instead, I pick her up and toss her over my shoulder.

"What are you doing now?" she shrieks from upside down as I carry her toward the bedroom.

"Taking you to bed. We should start practicing making a baby so we're ready when the time comes."

She laughs then lets out another shriek when I toss her onto the bed, watching her bounce twice. She shoves her hair out of her face then gets up on her elbows, watching me take off my shirt. "You're crazy."

I drop my shirt to the floor then climb on top of her, straddling her hips. "About you."

"And cheesy," she breathes, as I slide my hands up her waist, taking her shirt off.

"Mmm." I dip my head to her chest and nip her hard nipple through her bra, listening to her moan. She arches up into me, and I slip my hands around her back, unhooking her bra then sliding it down her shoulders. When she's exposed to me from the waist up, I cup both of her breasts and look into her heated eyes. "You're tits are perfect."

I squeeze them both then latch onto one nipple while I pull the other between my fingers. She writhes under me and my cock jerks. I move my knees between her thighs and unhook the button on her jeans. When I get them and her panties off, I skim my hands up her legs. "Spread for me baby, wanna see that cunt," I urge, and she does.

I use my thumbs to open her up completely then lean forward, placing my mouth on her sex. Her fingers latch onto my hair and her hips jerk off the bed as she gasps. Sweet, even between her legs, she's sweet. I eat her, listening to her moan my name, then slowly thrust two fingers inside her. When she clamps down around them, I groan, leaning back to look at her.

"Wanna feel that on my cock, baby. You need to come so you can give me what I want."

179

"Okay," she pants, urging me forward with her hand still in my hair.

I grin at her then lean forward and suck her clit into my mouth, keeping my fingers steady. When I flick her clit and rub her G-spot, she comes and more of her sweetness fills my mouth. I kiss her inner thigh as she falls back to the bed, and then get up and unhook my jeans. She gets up on her knees, and as soon as my cock springs free, she wraps her warm, soft hand around it.

"Whatcha doing, baby?" I hiss out as she strokes me from root to tip. She doesn't answer; what she does is better. Her full lips close around the tip and she bobs, taking me fully into her mouth. "Fuck." I hold her hair back and watch myself disappear while she uses her hand and mouth in the perfect rhythm. Her eyes meet mine and I run my fingers along the edge. "You look beautiful like this. Beautiful with your mouth full of me." She moans around my length, and the vibration sends a jolt down my spine. "As much as I want to watch you swallow me down, you're going to have to show me that another time. When I come, I'm coming inside your pussy."

Her pupils dilate and I watch her hand disappear between her legs as I speak. I almost lose it, almost shoot off right then at the sight of her getting herself off while taking me down her throat. "Fuck, you gotta stop baby." My head falls back to my shoulders when she flicks her tongue over the tip of my cock. She doesn't stop; she sucks me harder and faster. "Jesus," I hiss, somehow finding the strength to pull her mouth off me, which is torture.

"Cobi." Her eyes meet mine, her expression turned on and frustrated.

"Quiet." I spin her around and shove her shoulders forward into the bed then move between her legs. I thrust my hand between her thighs and cup her over her drenched sex while I wrap my other hand around my cock. "Do you want me?"

I lean over her and she nods, licking her lips. Moving my hand, I take hold of her hip then slide into her slowly. "I love this ass," I growl as my hands roam over her backside, and she moans.

I know what she wants, know what gets her off, but I don't give it to her right away. I keep my strokes slow and let my hands glide across her warm skin. I wait until she's least expecting it then bring my hand down on one cheek. She moans, her pussy spasms, and her head arches back toward her shoulders. I glide my hands over her again and wait before I smack the opposite cheek. The response is the same, only this time her pussy doesn't just spasm; it ripples and pulls me deeper. My balls get tight and my spine tingles. I'm close, so fucking close. I want to come, but never want to come, just so I can keep fucking her. It's like heaven and hell and I can't get enough.

I lean over her, wrap my arm under her breasts, and bring her up to her knees. Once I've got her where I want her, I cup her breast. "Touch yourself, baby. Then you and I are going to come together."

She doesn't hesitate. She slides her fingers between her legs and I know the instant they move over her clit, because a soft whimper escapes her lips. I move my mouth to her neck and fuck her hard. When she starts to come, I bottom out deep inside her and let her pull me over the edge with her. I come, biting into her soft flesh while stars dance in my vision. My heart pounds, and my breathing is labored as I kiss her neck over the spot I just bit.

"You okay?"

"I think I might like this practice business," she pants, and I laugh. She turns her head and her soft eyes meet mine. "I love your laugh, and really love hearing you do it while you're still inside me."

"I just love being inside you." I rub my cheek against hers when she smiles then move my eyes to her shoulder. "I bit you."

"I know." She tips her head down to look at the mark. "I thought I was going to come while coming when you did that." She grins at me, and I laugh once more. Fuck, when have I ever laughed this much? I don't think I ever have. Then again, I've never met another woman like her. I pull out of her then gather her in my arms and fall back onto the bed with her against my chest, closing my eyes. "Can we take a bath?" she asks, sounding hopeful, and I smile.

"Yeah, as soon as I can move to get up." I open one eye to look at her. "You just about killed me."

"Liar." She leans up, kissing my jaw, then starts to pull away.

"Where are you going?" I catch her hand before she can get off me.

"I'm going to start the bath. I'll be right back."

I release her then listen to the bath start up. When it does, my cock starts to get hard once more just thinking about what we did the last time we were in the bath together.

On that thought, I get up and head to the bathroom, and once again we make a mess and soak the floor. Not that I can find it in me to give a fuck.

"Are you sure you really want me coming along with you guys?" Hadley asks into the phone while picking up her glass of orange juice and taking a sip. "I know, but I don't want to impose. Really, we can plan something for another time," she tries again, and her eyes meet mine. When I smile and shrug, she lets out a small, frustrated huff.

She's been on the phone for the last fifteen minutes trying to get out of going out with my cousins tomorrow night. She's also been failing horribly, mostly because she's talking to Willow, Harmony's sister. Willow has never been one to be put off or deterred when she wants something, and she wants Hadley in the family fold. Really, all my family does, which is why they're constantly inviting her out to lunch or over for coffee. She's also had my female cousins over here a few times since she moved in two weeks ago, and even though I know she's not used to having a big family, I know she's enjoying it.

"Okay, if you're sure, then I'll go." She looks up at me and her eyes widen at whatever Willow is saying. "Uh... yeah, okay. Umm, no, I've never been to one before." Her cheeks darken, and I wonder what that's about. "Would you mind if I invited Brie? You know, since she's getting married in a few months. Awesome. Got it, seven. We'll meet you guys at the restaurant then go from there. Thanks, you too. See you then." She hangs up and ducks her head.

"What's going on?" I ask as she pushes her scrambled eggs around on her plate, looking nervous for some reason.

"Oh nothing." Her cheeks get darker, which makes me even more curious.

"Why are you turning red like you do when I talk about sex?"

"I'm not," she denies, avoiding looking at me.

"You are. What are you guys doing?"

Her eyes meet mine. "Apparentlywearegoingtoamalestripclub."

"What?" I frown, having no idea what she just said, because it was all garbled together.

"We're going to look at penises."

"Did you just say you're going to look at penises?" I question, knowing I must have heard her wrong.

I didn't. She starts to nod.

"Willow wants to surprise your recently married and engaged cousins with a penis viewing."

"You're shitting me," I growl, staring at her in disbelief.

"I'm going to invite Brie." She shrugs, taking a bite of eggs, suddenly seeming totally okay with this conversation.

"You're not going, so no, you're not going to invite Brie anywhere."

"I told Willow I would. I tried to get out of it, which you heard, but she was adamant I go. So now I'm going, and since Brie is getting married soon, I'm going to invite her to go look at penises too."

"Can you stop saying the word penises?" I scrub my hands down my face. I can't believe this shit.

"What do you want me to call them?" She smirks, and I narrow my eyes on her mouth.

"I don't want you to call them anything. Fuck, why did I think it was a good idea to encourage you to be friends with the women in my family?"

"I don't know, but it was your idea, so this is basically all your fault."

"You're not going out with them," I repeat once more.

"Yeah, I am."

"No you fucking are not, Hadley."

"Okay then, I won't go." She shrugs, picking up her juice and taking another sip.

I study her for a long moment, trying to read if she's really agreeing, but her face and eyes are blank. "You're still going, aren't you?"

"Yep." She takes another sip from her glass then sets it down. "Besides, penises are weird looking, so it's not like I'm going to be getting off on looking at them. So you have nothing to worry about. And hello?" She waves her hand out toward me. "I don't need a man since I've got you."

"Penises are weird looking?" I repeat, stuck on her earlier statement.

"Have you looked at your penis?" she questions, dropping her eyes briefly to where my penis is out of sight under the table. "Don't get me wrong. It's a great penis, the best around, but it's still weird looking."

"Thanks, baby," I mutter sarcastically.

"Anytime, honey." She grins.

"You're not going." I sound like a fucking broken record.

"You keep saying that like you have a say, when you don't. You can't tell me what to do."

"You're mine, so yes I fucking can."

She tips her head to the side, and I see the wheels spinning. "Have you ever been to a strip club?"

"Not since I've been with you."

"So you have been to one?"

"Again, not since I've been with you," I repeat.

She slides back from the island and stands. "Exactly how mad are you going to be at me tomorrow night when I get home?"

"Furious," I answer, feeling my jaw get hard.

"That works," she says, taking her plate to the sink.

"It works for you that I'm gonna be pissed?" I ask in disbelief.

"No, but I'm curious about angry sex with you." She grins at me over her shoulder, and my cock twitches behind my zipper.

"I can show you now, since I'm already close to losing my fucking mind."

"As much as I want that experience, I've got to get to work," she singsongs, going toward the bedroom. When she's out of sight, I pull in a breath, pick up my phone, and send out a few texts, hoping I can shut this shit down. When I'm done, I drop my phone to the counter and follow her into the bathroom, where I have my way with her bent over the vanity. It's not angry sex, but it's still fucking hot.

Chapter 16

"THERE ARE SO MANY penises!" I shout over the loud music, and all the girls look at me and start to laugh. "Seriously, I can't look anywhere without seeing one. Why do they have to be so weird looking?"

"Right?" December agrees, and I look her way, seeing her face is the same color red as mine probably is. "I don't understand any of this." She looks to the side and cringes when one of the guys bumps into her from behind.

"Stop being such a prude," April, December's sister, shouts and shoves a handful of cash in the direction of one of the guys who's dancing close by. He grins at her, taking that as an invitation to thrust his hips in her direction. When she doesn't acknowledge the thrusting, he moves on to another woman, who's all too eager to have him in her space.

My nose scrunches up. "I don't get it. They are just guys, naked guys. What's the big deal?" I look around, trying to figure out what the fuss is about. The room is packed full of women, women of all different ages, shapes, and races. The one thing they have in common is they're all going insane. Some holding out money, some tossing money into the air, most of them screaming like they're fourteen and these guys are their favorite boy band.

"Don't try to figure it out," Brie says, and I glance over to see her casually taking a sip of her drink. "Just enjoy the show for what it is."

"I'm a little disappointed," I tell her, looking around again while trying to avoid looking at any penises—something that is hard to do, since they seem to be everywhere. "This isn't even a show, I mean, in the movie *Magic Mike,* the guys at least did a little performance. This is just penis chaos."

"Yep," she agrees, then asks, "How was Cobi when you left the house tonight?"

"Mad, but then again, he's been mad since yesterday." I smile. "Though I kind of like him mad, so there's that."

"I bet." She grins, and I grin back.

"I don't know if I'm cut out for this," July states, plopping down next to Brie and me in our booth.

"You either, huh?" December questions.

"I didn't even want to come at all, but when Wes told me I wasn't *quote-unquote allowed to*, I had to come to prove a point that he's not my boss." She looks around and cringes when she sees a guy's erection not far from her face. "I don't think this is worth the fight I'm sure Wes and I are going to have tonight when I get home."

I feel for her, because I'm sure I will be having that same fight with Cobi. I just hope angry sex with him is worth it. Who am I kidding? All sex with Cobi is awesome.

"This is insane," Ashlyn says, shoving her way through two women to get to us, holding a bottle of water in her hand that she obviously got from the bar across the room. "Seriously, you'd think these women have never seen a dick before."

"I think the point is they *need* to see a dick," April chimes in from above us, and I tip my head back to look at her. "Not everyone here is getting laid regularly like you all are."

Having met April a few times, her bluntness doesn't surprise me anymore. It's so odd, having met all of Cobi's family, just how different everyone is, yet how accepting everyone is of each other. Like December and April—they're sisters, but couldn't be more opposite.

Where December is reserved and shy, April is aggressive and forward to the extreme, yet you know when you see them interact that they love each other.

"I really think I might need to leave. I'm starting to get claustrophobic," December states, moving away from one of the guys when he starts to dance close to her. "And I think I've seen enough penises tonight to last me a lifetime. Actually, I think I might need therapy before I ever willingly look at a penis again."

"I wouldn't mind getting out of here either," I say to December, and her eyes fill with relief.

"You guys can't go," Willow—who planned this whole fiasco—states, looking at each of us. "We just got here and it's still early."

"We're not far from downtown. What if we catch a cab to Broadway and hit some of the bars?" I suggest, really hoping they all say yes.

"I'm good with that," December says, smiling at me.

"Oh all right," Willow gives in. "But I'm going to see if my friend Curtis can get us on one of the party bikes."

"Do you mean those carts you have to pedal while drinking?" I ask for confirmation, and she nods while pulling out her phone.

"I don't know if that's a good idea," July says, and Willow glances up from her phone.

"Why not?"

"What happens when all of us get too drunk to pedal?"

"Don't worry about that. It will be fun."

"Famous last words," Brie inserts, and I look at her and smile.

"All set, Curtis has a bike for us." Willow stands.

April, who hasn't been in on the conversation, frowns at us as we all stand. "We're leaving already?"

"We're going down to Broadway."

"Cool, then." She leads all of us through the crowd and out the door of the club. When we get outside, we get two cabs and head for Broadway. After that, the night is mostly a blur of pretending to pedal, drinking too much, and laughing so hard my stomach hurts.

I wake up slightly disoriented, and groan when I hear Cobi chuckle and feel the bed move with the sound. What could he possibly think is funny when my head is pounding and my stomach is twisting is anyone's guess.

"I'm guessing from that sound you don't feel so good."

"Please don't talk." I pull my pillow over my head to try to block him and the light seeping through my eyelids out.

"You won't feel better until you get some food in your stomach and take something for your head."

Even the mention of food makes my stomach roll. "I'm good. I just need to sleep."

"It's three in the afternoon. You've been asleep since I picked you up last night and put you in my truck."

Wait what? I don't remember that. I pull the pillow away and look at him. "You picked me up last night?"

"You called and said you were ready to come home and have angry sex."

Okay. Apparently, I shouldn't drink so much ever again, because I don't remember doing that.

"Thanks for coming to get me."

"Anytime, baby." He touches his lips to mine.

"You seem okay," I observe.

"Do you mean I don't seem pissed?" he asks with a grin, and I nod. "I'm not mad. I know you guys didn't stay in the club long. I also know you were having fun after you left, so it's all good."

I frown. "You know we didn't stay long? How do you know that?" I question.

"I have my ways."

My frown gets deeper. "Did you follow us?" He shrugs and I sit up. "Seriously?"

"With shit that's gone down recently, I needed to make sure you were okay."

"But following us?"

"Did I intrude?" *No, he didn't, but still....* "No, I let you do your thing and kept an eye on you from a distance. You didn't even know I was around."

"Your insanity knows no bounds," I whisper, looking into his eyes.

"You're mine to protect and to take care of."

"I like how you make being insane seem so rational." I roll my eyes then cover my face when the action hurts my head.

"Go get in the shower. I'll make you something to eat and get you some pills." He kisses the top of my head then gets off the bed.

"Just so you know, when I'm not feeling like I might die, we're going to continue this conversation."

"Just so you know, everything I do, crazy or not, is because I love you, baby, with everything I am."

My body gets warm and my heart melts. "Don't be sweet when I'm annoyed with you."

"Get your beautiful ass up so I can feed you," he orders.

My eyes move over him and I sigh. He looks way too hot wearing just a pair of black running bottoms and nothing else.

I want to say something sassy in return, but nothing comes to mind, so I just pick up one of the pillows from the bed next to me and toss it in his direction. It doesn't even come close to hitting him, and he laughs as he leaves the room. Maxim wanders in the open door, and when he sees I'm up sitting on the bed, he jumps up next to me and licks the side of my face.

"Hey, buddy." I rub his head, and he rests his weight against me, causing me to fall back against the mattress. I laugh, pushing him away so I can get up, and his whole bottom half wobbles and shakes with excitement as he stands on the bed. "I need a shower, big guy. We'll play after I get out."

He lets out a loud woof then bounds off the bed and out of the room. I head into the bathroom and go right to the shower, turning it on. When I get to the sink to brush my teeth, I gasp at my appearance. I look ready for Halloween. My hair looks like I stuck my finger in a light socket, my eye makeup is smeared down under my eyes onto my cheeks, my face is pale, and the red lipstick I wore last night is smeared across my mouth.

"Beautiful," I huff in disbelief, grabbing a wipe to clean the residue of makeup off my face. "He's so full of it."

"Talking to yourself is a sign of mental instability."

I jump in place then glare at Cobi where he's leaning against the doorjamb, watching me.

"I'm just reminding myself that you truly are crazy."

"How's that?" His lip twitches, and he crosses his ankles, then his arms over his chest like he's settling in for a show.

"Do you not see my face?" I stop scrubbing to place my hands on my hips.

His eyes sweep my hair, face, and then down to his T-shirt he obviously put me in last night, and his eyes are darker when they meet mine once more. "What?"

"I look like I'm ready to step on the set of *The Walking Dead*," I point out the obvious, while lifting my hands to wave in the direction of my face.

He shrugs. "You're still beautiful."

"And I see you're still crazy." I go back to scrubbing, while asking, "Is my breakfast ready?"

"Yeah, it's in the microwave so Maxim doesn't eat it," he says, shoving his hands into the waist of his pants and then kicking them off toward the closet. My mouth instantly waters at the sight of him completely naked.

"Are you showering with me?" I know my tone is hopeful, just like I know my nipples are tight and my core is suddenly hot and wet.

"Yeah."

Yay! my mind screams, my headache and nausea nowhere in sight.

His gaze on mine heats then he curses under his breath and looks away, shoving his fingers through his hair. "As much as I want what you're offering, baby, I gotta get to work."

"No." I pout like a child who was forced to walk down the candy aisle at the grocery store and not pick anything up. "Seriously?"

"I'll make it up to you." He comes toward me, grabbing the face wipe out of my hand and tossing it to the counter. Then, with his hands on my hips, he walks me backward to the shower, stripping his shirt up and over my head. He opens the shower door, and as soon as we're closed inside, his mouth covers mine and his fingers slide between my legs. Like he always does, he takes care of me, which means when he leaves me in the shower to get ready for work, I've had two really great orgasms and still have a smile on my face.

Chapter 17

Sitting at my desk Monday morning, I stare at my computer monitor in disbelief then pick up my phone and put it to my ear. I call my boss, not Marian. I call the actual owner of Giving Hearts, Scott Rosenblum. It rings and goes to voice mail, and I leave a short message with my name, asking him to call me back as soon as he has time to talk. When I place the phone back in its holder, I rub the bridge of my nose.

Last Friday, I received a phone call from another one of my families who had funds go missing. Funds they were planning on using to help with their child's swimming fees. Knowing that Marian would give me the same runaround, I sent another letter to the company that takes care of the accounting, and this morning, I'm looking at almost the exact response I got before.

Dear Miss Emmerson,
Our records indicate that Check Number 2341 in
the amount of $222.45 was direct deposited on October 14th.
Please let us know if we can assist you further.
All the best.

This situation is really starting to frustrate me, and I can feel it in my gut that something is off. I look at the clock on the wall across the room and scoot away from my desk, opening the drawer where I keep my purse. I need to be across town in twenty minutes, which means I need to leave now. Thankfully, when I left Scott a message, I also gave him my cell number, and hopefully he calls me on that if he doesn't reach me at the office.

I shut down my computer, grab my purse, and then leave for my car, saying goodbye to a few co-workers on my way out.

I make it to the McKays' and park in their driveway, and as soon as I open my door, I hear kids laughing and shouting. I get out and slam my door, tucking my notebook and case file in my purse. It's a Monday, but most of the schools are out for fall break, so the sound of kids being kids isn't a surprise.

When I make it to the front door, and before I even have a chance to knock, it's swung open and Liz smiles at me. "We're in the kitchen making cookies." Her smile lights up her eyes, and some of the tension in my shoulders dissipates seeing her happy and not heartbroken over her dad. I follow her into the two-story brick house, looking around as she hop-skips away.

I drop my bag on the bench near the front door that's covered with backpacks, shoes, and random children paraphernalia, and then I shrug off my coat and hang it on one of the few unused hooks. Having been here before, I know that even though there's clutter covering the coffee table in the living room, even though there is unopened mail on the entryway table, and dust gathering on some of the unused surfaces, the things that really matter are in place, organized, happy, healthy, and clean. This is the home of a family with children. A family who enjoys spending more time together than they do making sure everything is perfect and in its place.

When I hit the kitchen and see all the kids gathered there, relief and joy washes over me.

"If you're quick, you might be able to get a cookie," Sarah McKay says, smiling while using a spatula to lift freshly baked cookies off a pan. With another family, I might think this exact moment was staged, but with Sarah, I know it's not; this is her life. This is who she is, the kind of mom she is.

"Thank you." I take a cookie when Eric holds one out to me and then take a bite. "How have things been?" I ask after I chew and swallow.

"Crazy as always," Sarah answers with a grin. Then she looks around at the kids in the kitchen. "Adult talk time, guys. Grab a cookie and head outside for a while." All the kids groan but leave, grabbing cookies on their way outside. When the door closes behind the last one, Sarah pulls her eyes off the door and looks at me. "They're happy. I know it's been on your mind, but I promise you they're happy here." She looks away, picking up the cookie sheet, placing it in the sink, and turning the water on over it before looking at me. "Things at first were a little confusing after they found out their dad wasn't coming back for a while, but they've both settled in and are coming to terms with things."

Relief hits me hard, and I take a seat on one of the stools around her kitchen island. Mr. Shelp is going away for a few years, five to be exact, and it's been difficult thinking that his children might have issues with their new normal, even if knowing they are better off now than they were when they were under his supervision.

"I'm glad to hear that," I say quietly.

"They're great kids, sweet kids." She pulls in a breath. "I know they miss their daddy, but they're both doing okay for right now."

"I'm happy to hear that." My response is instant. "If things change—"

"You know I'll call you," she cuts me off. "For now though, they are okay. They're settling in."

"Thank you. I wish..." I grab her hand across the counter between us. "I wish there were more people like you in the world. You might not know it, but you are making a difference."

Her face softens. "All I ever wanted was a big family. Each and every child who comes into our home gives me a little piece of my dream, no matter if they stay a month or forever."

Yes, I really, really wish more people were like the McKays. People who are just good people, people who are willing to give children a warm, safe place when they need it most.

After chatting and spending some time with each of the kids, I fill out my notes and schedule another visit. After I leave and get into my car, I check my phone, which was on silent while I was inside the house. I see a missed call from Scott, so I call him back and he answers on the third ring. While I drive back to the office, I tell him what happened Friday and about the email I got today. When he seems like he has no idea what I'm talking about, I mention Marcus and his missing money.

"Why hasn't Marian informed me of this situation?"

At his question, my stomach drops. "Pardon?"

"Why haven't I been informed of this situation until now?" The question is harsh, and in order not to run off the road, I have to pull over onto one of the side streets and park.

"I was under the impression that you did know about these issues." Bile crawls up the back of my throat. "Marian told me that she'd been working with you on finding out who's responsible, since this is not the first time funds have gone unaccounted for."

"Good Lord." He sounds worried— actually... freaked. "I'm going to have to call you back. I need to figure out what the fuck is going on."

"Okay," I say quietly.

I stare out the front windshield for a long time, trying to figure out what I'm feeling, what I'm going to do. I should have known not to trust Marian. I should have questioned what she was saying the moment I saw her in my office, and I sure as heck should have done more research after Reggie called me to tell me about Marcus's money.

"How the heck is she getting the money?" That, I do not know.

When I get back to the office, the parking lot is empty, so I know everyone is out. I use my key and let myself in and leave the door unlocked for anyone else who comes back. As soon as I get inside and reach my desk, I start up my computer. I search through all my files, looking for what exactly, I have no idea, but there has to be something I'm missing, some reason Marian was at my desk using my computer. So engrossed in what I'm doing when my cell phone rings, I almost jump out of my skin.

"Where are you?" Cobi barks into my ear before I even get a chance to say hello.

"At the office. Why? What's going on?" Worry that something happened to someone in his family makes me feel nauseous.

"Fuck," he clips, and I feel his anger like a physical touch even through the phone.

"What happened? Is everyone okay?"

"Are you alone?"

My heart rate spikes at his question, and I look out into the main office through the glass windows, seeing it's still empty. Or at least I think it is. Marian's door is closed and her blinds are pulled, and I can't see into the kitchen.

"I think so, but I can't see into the kitchen or Marian's office," I say, and he repeats what I just told him. Why is he repeating what I just told him?

"Where in the office are you exactly?"

"I'm in my office." My voice shakes.

"Do you have a closet or a bathroom in there?"

"Cobi, you're freaking me out. What's going on?" I whisper, my hands starting to tremble right along with my voice.

"I'll explain in a second. Right now, I need you to answer my question."

"No, no closet or bathroom." I listen to him repeat what I just said again. What is going on?

"I want you to get under your desk and pull your chair in behind you once you're under it."

"Cobi—"

"Do it now, baby. It's going to be okay, but I need you to listen to me."

I squat down under my desk and pull in my chair. As soon as I'm fully sitting on the floor, I try to take a breath but realize I can't.

"Breathe, just breathe. It's going to be okay." His soft words ease some of the tension in my lungs.

"Wh—s happ-ing," I wheeze. I can hear sirens through the phone.

"My lieutenant got a call from the owner of Giving Hearts not long ago, along with paperwork proving that your boss Marian has been going into clients' accounts and changing their deposit information to her own." Well, that answers how she's been getting the money. My eyes close. "We're on our way now to arrest her." *Oh my God.* "Just stay put. We have no reason to believe she's armed, but I'm not taking any chances."

Relief makes it easier to breathe and I take a few much-needed breaths. "I don't think she's here," I state quietly. "Her car wasn't in the lot when I got back from my clients house, and the building was locked. I used my key to get in."

"That's good, baby, but don't move from where you are," he says, just as I hear a familiar voice in the outer office.

"Brie's here." I push the chair away without a thought and scramble out from under the desk. I can hear Cobi shout at me to stay put from my cell, but I ignore him and my phone when it falls from my hand as I run to where I see Brie disappearing into the kitchen.

"Hey." She smiles at me, and I see she has her cell phone to her ear.

"Come on." I grab her hand and catch her frown before I turn and start pulling her toward my office.

"Ken, I'm going to call you back. Something is going on with Hadley. Yeah, love you too." She must hang up, because she forces me to stop. "What's going on?"

"I don't have time to explain. Right now, I just need you to come get under my desk with me."

"Hadley." Her voice is filled with worry.

"Now, Brie." I look up at her then spin when I hear the main office door open.

"You called Scott," Marian states as the door shuts behind her.

"Marian." I place myself in front of Brie and start pushing her back. "The police are on their way."

"What?" Brie gasps from behind me.

"They aren't on their way. They're outside," Marian turns the lock on the door. I look past her to the glass door, but I can't see anything outside.

"If you know that, then what are you doing?" I question, watching her dig in her bag.

"I'm not sure yet. I do know I'm not going to jail though." When her hand comes out, she's holding a leather case shaped like a gun. I see it *is* a gun when she unhooks a clasp, releasing the pink revolver from its holder.

"So you're going to shoot us?" My voice is filled with disbelief and fear.

Brie comes to my side and closes her hand around mine, saying quietly. "Marian, you need to put that away before you do something you'll regret."

"She should have just kept her nose where it belonged," she snaps at Brie, and then glares at me.

"Marian, please."

"Shut up, just shut up! I need to think." She waves the gun at us, and Brie and I tighten our hold on each other.

"It cannot be that bad. Whatever you did can't be worth hurting anyone," Brie says calmly.

"Do you have any idea how much time I'll get for stealing over five hundred thousand dollars?" she hisses, and my eyes widen.

"Holy fuck," Brie breathes.

I hear my cell ring and look toward my office, where I dropped it in my haste to get to Brie. Tears burn the back of my throat. I know Cobi's calling me, and I know he's probably furious I didn't listen to him and scared out of his mind right now.

"Why couldn't you just mind your own business?" I know she's talking to me, even though she's looking at the floor as she paces. "I was so close. So close to getting away, to disappearing." She stops, and her rage-filled eyes land on me. When she lifts the gun in her hand, stars start to fill my vision and my lungs get tight. "This is all your fault."

Frozen, all I can do is stare at her. "Don't do this." My lips move to say more, but no sound comes out.

I use Brie's hand still in mine to shove her to the ground as I hear the click of the trigger being pulled back and a loud popping sound. Chaos erupts as we hit the floor. The sound of glass shattering, another shot, and people shouting.

"Hadley!"

Cobi? I blink at his face above mine.

"Fuck, baby. Jesus." He pulls me against his chest and wraps his arms around me so tight it's hard to breathe.

"Brie?" I look around for her in a panic.

"She's okay."

"I'm okay!" My eyes land on her and close when I see that she doesn't even have a hair out of place.

"Baby." Cobi wraps his hand around my jaw, and my eyes open to meet his filled with turmoil.

"I'm okay." I pull in a breath then repeat, "I'm okay," before I burst into tears and hold onto him, shoving my face into his neck.

Chapter 18

I WATCH COBI TALKING on the phone a few feet away, wearing a dark gray thermal, jeans, and boots, with his badge clipped to his belt. He hasn't shaved in a couple of days, and the growth on his cheeks and chin makes him look even more handsome than his normal handsome. When I see him smile at something his mom says, warmth and happiness radiate through me.

It's been six months since he ignored orders and broke through the glass door at my office to get to me when he saw Marina's gun trained on me. Marina was shot not by Cobi but by Frank. The wound to her shoulder was bad enough that she needed surgery, but after a week in the hospital, she was transferred to jail, where she will be for a very long time.

Surprisingly, it wasn't me who had nightmares after everything that happened. For weeks afterward, Cobi would wake up in a cold sweat or shout out to me in his sleep. It killed me to see him suffering like that, but thankfully with time and talking things out the nightmares have gone away. Still, I feel his eyes on me all the time, like he thinks I might disappear—something that has only gotten worse the last three months since I found out I was pregnant.

No, we did not plan on having a baby, and I personally would have preferred to be married to him before we did get pregnant, but apparently birth control really is only ninety-nine percent effective. Not that I'm complaining. In all reality, I'm excited to start a family with him, but now that big wedding Cobi mentioned is in the works, because he's refused to let me put off marrying him until after our daughter is born. He doesn't want me showing without having his last name, and I'm okay with that.

My eyes drop to the bowl of brownie batter I'm mixing and catch on my engagement ring, a ring Cobi put on my finger two days before we found out we were having a girl. My not-so-simple, seriously over-the-top solitaire, three and a half-carat diamond ring took my breath away when Cobi slid it on my finger at his parents' house, where he had invited his family, Brie, and Kenyon to all celebrate with us after he asked me to be his wife.

"What are you making?"

I tip my head to the side to look at him as he slides his hand over my slightly pooched stomach, where our girl is growing. "I'm not sure," I respond, looking away from him and scooping out brownie batter over the layer of crushed graham crackers with melted butter I pressed into the bottom of the pan. "I wanted to try something new." He rests his chin on my shoulder and watches. "After this is done baking, I'm gonna add peanut butter and marshmallows on top then bake it again."

"Sounds good." He kisses my neck. I shiver, and my nipples pebble in response.

"Hopefully it tastes good." I fight back a moan as his hand comes up to close around my sensitive breast and his lips skim the shell of my ear. "I need to get it in the oven," I pant, but still press my ass into his length as he grinds against me.

He takes the pan off the counter and opens the oven, tossing it inside before slamming the door closed. "Done," he states, and I laugh as he turns me toward him and lifts me up, planting me on the counter. He shoves my legs apart, placing his hips between mine, then wraps his hand in my hair at the back of my skull and tips my head back until our eyes lock. "I love you."

"I love you too." My words end against his lips as he kisses me. I slide my hands up and under his shirt, feeling his warm skin over tight muscles. I keep pushing his shirt up until he pulls away and rips it off over his head. By the time he strips me of mine and removes my bra, I'm past the point of being turned on. I fumble with his belt as his hands go to my waist, and he grabs my leggings, ripping them down my hips and tossing them and my panties to the floor. I almost cry in relief when he pushes my hands away, unhooks his belt, and pulls his cock free.

"Ass to the edge, and spread wide, baby." He wraps one hand around my hip, the other around his length, stroking as I get closer to the edge. When I'm where he wants me, I wrap my hands around his biceps and his eyes drop between my legs. He watches as he slides the tip over my clit and back down, again and again, the sensation feeling like torture.

"Cobi." His head lifts and our eyes lock. "Please." My breath leaves on a whoosh. My hands move from his biceps and slide back to the counter behind me to hold me up as he finally gives me what I want, filling me in one long stroke.

"This what you want?" I nod, unable to speak as he slowly pulls out then slams back in. I lift my legs and wrap them around his back, keeping him close as my head falls back to my shoulders. "Swear, your pussy is so hot it's gonna burn me alive one of these days," he growls, moving his hand from my hip and sliding his thumb over my clit, making me jump from the added stimulation.

Since becoming pregnant, it doesn't take much for me to orgasm. It's like all of my nerve endings are closer to the surface and one touch can send me over the edge.

"Too much." I lock my eyes with his. "It's too much." My core tightens almost painfully around his length, but he doesn't ease up; he keeps rolling my clit while hitting my G-spot with each deep stroke. "Oh!" My arms fall away and my back lands against the counter as I come.

I feel his hands wrap around my inner thighs, keeping me open, using them to pull me into his thrust. My body trembles, and his strokes turn uneven before he plants himself deep, holding his hips flush against mine as he comes. When he drops his forehead to my chest, I slide my fingers into his hair and smile when he kisses between my breasts.

"Swear, since you got pregnant, your pussy is hotter, wetter, and tighter." I tip my eyes down to look at the top of his head. "I have to fight myself from shooting off in you the moment I slide inside, and you just about kill me every time you orgasm and clamp down around me like a vise. I might just keep you knocked up forever," he says, and I use my hands still in his hair to force him to look at me.

"Are you saying it wasn't good before I was pregnant?"

"It's always good between us, baby, but if you felt what I do, you'd understand what I'm saying." He kisses my chest. "Sadly, you can't feel it, but trust me, it's really fucking good and seriously fucking hot."

"Whatever."

I know my cheeks are pink when his eyes wander over my face and he shakes his head. "It's different for you now too. You're about ready to come the moment you get my cock."

"Maybe you should stop talking now," I suggest, and he pulls me up in front of him. The sudden movement with him still inside me has my walls clenching down around him tightly and my hands flying to his chest to steady myself as shockwaves roll through my system.

"You were saying?" He smirks.

"Don't be annoying when I just had an orgasm," I snap, and he laughs, slowly pulling his hips from mine. I mewl at the loss of him and then wrap my legs and arms around him as he picks me up.

"I'll give you a make-up orgasm in the shower," he says, carrying me through the bedroom and into the bathroom.

"I don't have time for a make-up orgasm. I have brownies in the oven," I remind him, and my stomach rumbles.

"I'll be fast." He sets me on my feet and I narrow my eyes on him.

"When are you ever fast?" I ask, while he reaches in to start up the water. "The last time you told me we would be quick, we were an hour late to your parents' house.

"Babe," is all he says with a grin.

I roll my eyes. "It's true. You don't know how to be quick."

"Okay then, you'll be quick, and then you can make it up to me later."

"How did my make-up orgasm turn into me making it up to you?"

I ask, and then I lose my train of thought, because he distracts me with his hands and his mouth.

As promised, he makes me come quickly and not just once but twice. I get out of the shower just in time to pull my brownies from the oven, and after I add the peanut butter and marshmallows, we eat dessert naked in bed and it's delicious.

Cobi

I reach out for Hadley, and when I don't feel her in the bed with me, my eyes open to complete darkness. I get up on an elbow and look toward the bathroom. It's dark and the lights off, so she's not there. I sit up, tossing back the covers, move to the edge of the bed, and stand. I pull on a pair of sleep pants and leave the bedroom.

When I hit the living room and don't see her there or in the kitchen, I know exactly where she is. Somewhere she's been spending more and more time the last few months. I go to the door of what used to be my workout room/mostly junk room and lean against the doorjamb. She's sitting in the middle of the empty room on the floor with a book on her lap, scribbling inside it while Maxim sleeps next to the stack of boxes containing the crib and changing table I still need to put together.

I study her silently for a moment, something I tend to do a lot, like I need to remind myself she's real, that she's mine, and that I get to have her for the rest of my life. "I'm not a real big fan of waking without you in bed with me."

Her head comes up at the sound of my voice, and the instant her eyes meet mine, I'm struck by how much love I see shining brightly back at me.

"Sorry." She smiles, shrugging. "I couldn't sleep, so I got up and somehow ended up in here writing in her book."

"You should have woken me up."

"You need sleep." She closes the book and then sets it aside. "Since you're here, do you mind helping me up?"

I push away from the door and go to her, taking both her hands. I pull her up against me and kiss the top of her head. "What did you add to her book this time?"

"Just things about how I'm feeling, what I'm craving, stuff like that." As she speaks, I move my hands from her hips and rest them over her stomach. The nightgown she's wearing is one from before she was pregnant, so the soft cotton is stretched over her breasts and pregnant belly that's becoming more noticeable by the day.

"Are you nervous about tomorrow?" I lift my gaze to hers.

"You mean the whole marrying you thing we're doing? No." Her eyes search mine. "Why are you nervous about tomorrow?"

"I'm not the one who couldn't sleep," I remind her gently.

She laughs. "Your daughter might only be the size of an avocado, but I swear she's sitting right on my bladder. I got up to pee eight times before I finally gave up on sleep and came in here." She waves her hand around, and I follow the movement with my eyes.

"After we get back from our honeymoon, Dad and I will paint, get the furniture set up, and we'll pick you out a chair so you're not sitting on the floor."

"I like it in here." She chews the inside of her cheek. "I know it's weird, but I feel close to her when I'm in here. Even with it empty, I feel closer to her."

"It's not gonna be empty for long. Before you know it, she'll be here."

"I know." She yawns.

"Let's get you to bed. You have important business to tend to tomorrow, so you need your rest."

She snorts. "Between your mom and Brie, I won't be allowed to lift a finger. I was told my only job is to show up and look pretty."

"I love the way they think." I swing her up in my arms and carry her to the bedroom. Once I place her in bed, I get in with her and curl my body around hers, resting my hand over our daughter.

"Are you excited?" she asks as I kiss her bare shoulder, and she laces her fingers with mine resting over her stomach.

"About marrying you? Yeah."

"No, about our daughter," she corrects softly, and I smile against her skin.

When she told me she was pregnant, I was shocked but knew there was a plan in the works that was bigger than her or me. I won't lie; I wish we had a little more time just the two of us, because I'm selfish when it comes to her, but I'm looking forward to becoming a father. I'm excited I'm having a girl, even if I am a little nervous about what that means for my future. My parents and family are also excited for us and looking forward to adding another baby to our ever-growing family, and my sister is planning to be here for a month after the birth to spend some time with her niece and new sister-in-law.

"Are you?" Her hand tightening on mine reminds me of her question.

"I can't wait to meet her. I can't wait to see you as a mom, and I'm looking forward to our future together and watching our family grow. So yeah, I'm excited."

I listen to her yawn again then laugh when she groans loudly. "I'll be right back." She gets off the bed and rushes to the bathroom. When I don't hear her getting sick—something that happens on occasion—I relax. The water goes on then off, and a moment later, she comes back and gets into bed, curling herself around me.

"'Night, baby," I whisper to the top of her head.

She doesn't respond, because she's already fallen asleep. With one hand resting on her stomach, the other curved around her back, I fall asleep with my entire world within my grasp.

December

I watch the happy couple enter the ballroom, along with everyone else, and smile when my cousin lifts his new wife's hand in the air, grinning huge before he spins her around to face him. When he has her where he wants her, he dips her back over his arm and kisses her. Everyone applauds and laughs, including me. I'm happy for him, but happier for Hadley. Over the last few months, we've gotten really close, and I know from her past that she deserves her happily ever after more than most people do.

"I wonder who's next," my sister April says, and I look over at her, feeling myself frown.

"What?"

"I wonder who's next. You know—the next person who's going to fall in love. It seems to be happening at an alarming rate." She takes a drink from her beer and glances around. "I'm saying not it. I have no desire to be shot at or kidnapped just to find love."

"You're so dramatic." I shake my head at her.

"Am I?"

Okay, she's not. There seems to be a theme when it comes to anyone with the Mayson last name falling in love. But still.

"Are you going to drink?" she asks, changing the subject and studying the glass of water in my hand.

"Probably not." I move to one of the tables that is set up around the dance floor and take a seat, smiling at a few people I know who are already sitting down.

"Good, you get to be my DD for the night," she says, sitting in the seat next to mine.

"Great," I sigh, not really looking forward to babysitting her all night to make sure she doesn't do anything stupid. I love my sister, but she tends to push the boundaries of stupid.

"Who's that?"

I look in the direction her eyes are pointed, and the world around me seems to come to a standstill. Across the room, talking to my cousin Sage and Brie's husband Kenyon, is a guy. Not just a guy, but the most gorgeous guy I have ever seen in my life. He's tall, taller than Sage, and almost as tall as Kenyon, who's practically a giant compared to everyone. His dark brown hair is longer on top and clipped short on the sides. He's in profile, so I can't see all of his face, but his jaw, covered in a rough-looking beard, is all sharp edges and straight lines. He has tattoos peeking out from above the edge of his collared shirt, and more on his thick forearms that I can see where his sleeves are rolled up to his elbows. His arms are so huge I doubt I could wrap both my hands around one of his biceps.

When he turns his body in my direction and smiles at something Sage says, my breath catches. I thought he was handsome in profile, but I was wrong. Straight on, his look is captivating and mysterious, with thick brows over his dark eyes and full lips surrounded by his beard.

"Whoever he is, I'm taking him home tonight," my sister says, and my stomach plummets. "God, he's hot. I can't wait to."

I swallow the sudden unexpected jealousy I'm feeling and really wish I hadn't agreed to be her DD, because I don't just need a drink; I need a whole bottle of tequila right now.

"Don't do anything stupid," I hiss, cutting her off and catching her gaze.

"Getting laid is not stupid. You'd know that if you ever tried it once in a while."

I bite my tongue to keep myself from saying something mean then look around the room for a place to escape. The sign for the restroom is like a neon flashing light catching my attention. I get up. "I'll be back," I mumble, before I scurry away with my head down and my heart lodged in my throat.

Since growing up, my sisters and I have had a rule. If one of us likes a guy, he's completely off limits, even if he's not interested in whoever has a crush on him. That rule has saved us on more than one occasion, but now I wish the stupid rule didn't exist. When I get to the restroom, I go to one of the stalls and stand there trying to get myself under control.

I know April, know she's probably already made a move to talk to whoever he is, and know without a doubt that he will be interested, because I have never met a guy who isn't interested in her. She's beautiful, funny, and outgoing—three things I am not. I'm cute enough, can be funny when I'm with my friends or family, but it takes time for me to warm up to people I don't know. I'm also the opposite of outgoing. I prefer books and laziness to getting out and having adventures. I have always been the same way.

After I know I'm not going to do something crazy like punch my sister in the face, I leave the bathroom and start to head toward the bar, figuring one glass of wine won't hurt. I place my order with the bartender then lean into the wood bar top with my forearms.

"You're Sage's cousin, right?" a deep voice asks, and my hair stands on end while butterflies take flight in my stomach.

I don't have to look to know it's him speaking. Still, I tip my head way back to catch his gaze. Lord, save me. He's tall and so beautiful.

I thought I got that from across the room, but seeing him up close is something else.

"I think he told me you were." His brows draw together over his dark eyes surrounded by thick lashes as I stare at him.

I mentally slap myself and force my mouth to start working. "Yes, I'm December."

His brow relaxes and he leans into the bar next to me with his hip, crossing his arms over his chest. "Another month." His eyes twinkle with humor.

"Pardon?"

"Met a July, June, May, and April. Now, December."

At the mention of April, my stomach twists. "Our parents were keeping with a theme." I pick up my wine and take a very unladylike gulp. Why didn't I see him first?

"Gareth." His hand comes my way. I don't want to take it, really don't want to, but my manners force me to place my hand in his. When his rough, warm strength envelops my hand, my breath sticks in my lungs. "It's nice to meet you."

I lick my lips, and whisper, "You too." With my hand still held in his, his gaze searches mine. The intense look in his eyes makes me feel funny, makes me feel like he sees some part of me I don't even know about.

"I thought you weren't drinking." My eyes close, blocking out Gareth, as April suddenly tosses her arm around my shoulders. "You're such a rebel, drinking wine when you're supposed to get me home safely."

"It's just one glass. I'll be fine to drive you home later." I open my eyes and turn my head to look at her.

"I know," she agrees, looking at me, and then she looks at Gareth and smiles. "My sister is a good girl. She always follows the rules."

God, I really wish that weren't true.

Hadley

Epilogue

WITH CHLOE FINALLY LATCHED onto my breast, I study her beautiful little face while gently rocking her. At just five days old, we're still in the process of *me* getting used to breastfeeding, and *her* taking my breast. It's been a learning curve, but I can honestly say there is something beautiful about having her take whatever she needs from me.

When she's finally had her fill, I adjust my shirt before bringing her up to my shoulder and rubbing her back. I press my nose into the top of her head and breathe in her scent, closing my eyes. The rattle of dog tags catches my attention, and I smile when I see Maxim wander into the room. He's been a trooper the last few days, between spending time at Cobi's mom and dad's while I was in the hospital giving birth, and coming home to a baby eating up most of his parents' time.

"Hey, big guy," I say, and he sets his head on my lap then presses his nose into Chloe's leg for a couple of seconds before looking up at me. "I know it's going to take some getting used to, but you'll be okay."

I stop rubbing Chloe so I can scratch behind his ears, and then move my hand back to her when she lets out a cry. Maxim lifts his head from my lap, tipping it from side to side, studying her before going and lying down next to her crib with a long groan.

After Chloe has burped and gone to sleep, I lay her down in her crib and turn on the baby monitor so I can watch her while I'm in the kitchen. Maxim doesn't move from his spot next to her crib, but then again, when she's in there, he never does. When I make it to the kitchen, I see Cobi left the news playing on the TV before he left to run to the store. I don't change it; instead, I pour myself some orange juice, drink it, and then go to the couch. Taking the monitor with me, I set it on the coffee table before I lie down.

Cobi wanted us to move from the townhouse during my last trimester into an actual home with a yard, but I put my foot down and refused. The place is perfect for us, and just the right amount of rooms. I know that eventually we will build a house on the piece of property his parents deeded out to him and me as a wedding gift, but I don't want to move before then. This place holds special memories for me, memories filled with falling in love and building a family. These walls hold our story, and even though I know we will eventually grow out of this place, I'm not ready to let it go just yet.

I feel fingers trail down the side of my face and open my eyes, sitting up quickly. "It's okay, just wanted to let you know I'm back," Cobi says, and I notice he has Chloe resting in the crook of his tattooed arm.

"Did she wake up?" I ask, feeling like a horrible mom if she woke up and I didn't hear her.

"No, saw you asleep, went to check on her, and couldn't resist picking her up." He gives me a sheepish smile.

"I think we're spoiling her." I run my fingers across her cheek, and her lips pucker in response.

"And I don't think I care," he responds, looking down at her for a moment before lifting his eyes to mine. "I'll always spoil my girls." My face gets soft and I lean over Chloe and press my lips to his jaw. When I pull away, I touch my fingers to where my lips were.

"We love you," I whisper.

"I know," he whispers back.

He thinks he does, but he really has no idea the way I feel for him. I love him, but every time I see him with our daughter, and how devoted he is to her, I know I *love* him. He's given me everything along with the proof that love is worth fighting for.

Cobi

A couple of months later . . .

I wake when I feel the bed shift, and watch Hadley through the darkness get up and leave the room. I start to sit up, but stop when I hear her through the baby monitor still sitting on my nightstand.

I listen, staring at the ceiling, as she talks to Chloe before starting to sing quietly. Since the day we brought Chloe home from the hospital, Hadley has jumped every time Chloe's made the smallest noise. Always rushing to pick her up before I even have the chance to. I thought with a little time she'd relax, but she hasn't, and it's started to worry me. I know she doesn't want to be anything like her mom was, and she's not. She's an amazing mom, devoted, loving, and beyond patient.

When her singing comes to an end, I get up and head out of the room. When I make it to the door to the nursery, I spot Maxim next to the crib asleep then lean against the jamb as my wife places our sleeping daughter in her bed. When she spots me after lifting her head, her expression shifts and pure love shines from her eyes.

I hold out my hand, and when she takes it, I pull her against me. "I would have gotten up with her, baby."

"I know." She smiles. "But unfortunately, you're not equipped with what she needed."

"I would have brought her to you," I say as I lead her to our room. Once we're both in bed, I drag the blankets over us and pull her against my side. I wait until she's settled before I speak. "You're a good mom."

"What?"

I feel her move, and tip my head down to look into her eyes with the light coming in from the street. "You're a good mom, a great mom, baby, but you're not a single parent forced to do it all alone," I tell her, feeling her body get tight against mine.

"I know," she says quietly, lifting up and placing her hands against my abs. "I just want her to know I'm here. That if she needs me, I'm right there with her. I never want her to question that. Question if I love her. I don't want her to ever feel alone."

Fuck. My muscles under her palms get tight, and "Baby" rips from my chest. "She knows. She'll never doubt that." I give her a squeeze. "Ever."

"But what if she does? What if—"

"She's going to grow up surrounded by love," I cut her off. "Surrounded by a family and parents who love her. She won't question that, and she will never—not ever—feel alone."

"I just love her so much," she says quietly.

"I know you do, and so do I. I also love you and want to help, so please let me do that."

"Okay," she agrees, dipping her head to touch her mouth to mine.

Before she can lean back, I slide my hand into her hair to keep her where she is. "Slip off your nightie and panties, baby. I'm gonna eat you then you're gonna ride me."

Her breathy "Okay" is filled with desire and need. As she pulls off her nightie and rolls to her side to slide her panties down her legs, I kick off my pajama bottoms then hook her around the waist, placing her over my face, her thighs on either side of my head.

Her hands slap against the headboard and "Oh" rushes from between her lips. I wrap my hands up and around her thighs then pull her down to my mouth. I groan when her wetness hits my tongue then go at her, licking, sucking, nibbling until her hips start jerking in my grasp, telling me she's close to losing it. I don't let up until she cries out and her head falls to rest on the headboard.

Hard as a rock, I wrap one hand around my length and stroke to ease the pressure. Hadley moves, and I adjust with her, holding onto her hip as she lowers herself down on my length. Her wet, tight heat closes around me, slowly making my teeth grind together. "Fuck, but I love this goddamn pussy," I groan when I'm fully seated within her.

"I love you," she moans, raising her hips and dropping them slowly. "I love the way you fill every inch of me. God, I feel you everywhere." Her head falls back and her eyes close. I lean up, capture her nipple between my lips, and roll my tongue over the tightly drawn tip. When her head tilts forward, our eyes lock.

I transfer my mouth to her other nipple, and her thighs around mine tighten while her pussy ripples along my length. "Do not come, Hadley, not until I say." Her eyes flare and her lashes flutter. "Christ, my wife is gorgeous when she's taking my cock." She mewls, coming down harder as I buck up into each and every downward stroke. When my balls draw tight, I slide my hand around her hip and roll my thumb over her clit. "Come with me, baby. Give it to me."

She clamps down around me, and I hold her still as I lose myself deep inside her. Breathing heavy, my heart pounding against my ribcage, I soak in our connection, the feel of her breath hitting my neck and her soft, warm body limp against mine. I close my eyes. Never could I have imagined a more perfect woman for me than her. She's every hope, dream, and wish mixed into the perfect package.

"If I was able to design the perfect wife, perfect mother, perfect woman, I still wouldn't even come close to describing you," I whisper against the side of her head, and her muscles contract. "Every day, I'm thankful that I get to wake up to you. That I get to spend the rest of my life with you at my side." I wrap my arms around her back, holding her flush against me. "Chloe is gonna feel the same every day of her life." Her body bucks against mine and I place my mouth to her ear. "You're everything to us, baby... fucking everything."

I roll us face-to-face and hold her tightly as she cries until she eventually falls asleep. When Chloe wakes up and I hear her through the monitor sometime later, I go to her room and bring her back to our bed, resting her slight weight against my chest. I hold her and her mom in my arms and know without a doubt I have within my grasp something most people will never really understand, something beautiful, something rare, something worth cherishing. A family created from love.

Hadley

Years, and years, and years later . . .

"You're the one who decided she should get a car for her seventeenth birthday," I remind Cobi, as he shoves his fingers through his hair and stomps past the front window for the thousandth time in the last three hours. He started pacing approximately thirty seconds after Chloe left to go out on a double date.

"You agreed with me." He stops long enough to look at where I'm currently sitting on our couch, watching the TV and him.

"I was under the influence of your penis. I don't think that counts." He grins, but then it slips away and his eyes move over me then back to the window. "She's okay, honey. It's not even time for her curfew," I remind him as he goes back to pacing.

"I just want to know she's home safe."

"And she'll be home soon, but your pacing is not going to magically make her appear," I say, and he glares at me. "Come sit down." I pat the cushion next to me.

"If she didn't look like you, I wouldn't worry so much, but she looks just like you."

She doesn't look like me. She has my hair and build, but she has her dad's beautiful eyes and sweet personality. Really, I think she looks a lot like her grandma Liz.

"I see Daddy's still pacing," Briana, our fifteen-year-old daughter, comments as she comes into the living room, plopping down on the couch next to me. I giggle when she gives me a surprised look and then smiles. Our middle girl looks a lot like a mixture of Cobi and me, with her daddy's hair and my eyes.

"Is Chloe home yet?" Jace, our fourteen-year-old mini alpha, shouts from his bedroom upstairs, and Briana shouts back "No" before I hear his bare feet hit the hardwoods upstairs. I listen as he jumps down the stairs—I'm sure skipping three or four at a time. Something I tell him not to do all the time, something he does anyway, because apparently he can't help himself. Thankfully though, he's never broken anything doing it.

"You shouldn't have let her go, Dad," he says to Cobi as soon as he hits the living room.

Briana hisses, "Shut up, Jace."

"You shut up," he returns, glaring at his sister.

222

"Both of you, stop it," Cobi cuts in on a growl, and both of them clamp their mouths shut and look at their dad with wide eyes. "Do not tell each other to shut up. Got it?" He looks between the two of them.

"Yeah, Dad," Jace mumbles.

"Yes, Daddy," Briana says softly.

I fight back a smile and wrap my arm around Briana then touch my boy's face when he sits close to me on my other side.

"Can I make popcorn?" Jace asks after a few minutes of watching TV.

"Sure, honey," I reply, and he gets off the couch, walking past his father, who reaches out and pulls him into a hug that he returns instantly.

Jace is the spitting image of his dad from head to toe, but he will probably be taller, since he's already touching the top of his head to Cobi's chin, and so tall I have to look up at him even now.

"Bring me a beer on your way back, kid," Cobi orders, and Jace smiles at him before disappearing through the door.

"I cannot wait to start dating," Briana states, and her dad stops pacing long enough to give her a look that has us both cracking up.

Jace comes back in with a bowl of popcorn, handing his dad his beer before taking the seat next to me again. Briana and I both dig in, ignoring his comments about us eating it all. I watch my husband out of the corner of my eye, and when I see his broad shoulders relax, I know my oldest baby is home.

"Scoot, kid," he orders Jace, standing over where he's still sitting next to me.

"What?" Jace asks through a mouthful of popcorn.

Instead of repeating himself, he sits down between Jace and me, taking the bowl of popcorn and placing it on his lap.

"So you're going to pretend like you haven't been standing at the window since she left?" I guess, rolling my eyes at my husband while both kids on the couch with us laugh at him.

"Just act normal." He wraps his arm around my shoulders, pulling me firmly into his side.

I look up at him as he tips his head down, and announce, "You're crazy."

His response is to kiss me, and when he pulls away, I'm smiling.

"Hey, guys," Chloe says as soon as she walks into the room. I look at my beautiful girl, who's looking at her dad while shrugging off her coat. "I'm home, so you can stop worrying now."

"I wasn't worried," he lies, and I let out a laugh, feeling his arm tighten around me.

This is family. People who worry. People who care. People who will be there when you need them most, and even when you don't need them at all.

I look over my kids and into my husband's eyes, feeling blessed beyond reason. We have built a beautiful family together. A family built on a solid foundation of love and devotion. A family that will never question what love is or ever feel alone.

The End

Every time I type The End on another Until book, I have to take a moment to breathe and remind myself that it's not the actual end. Until November was my first book baby, and the Until Series is like going home for me. I love these characters, love their family, and I'm always excited to see what will happen next in their world. Just like you are. Thank you all so much for loving the Maysons as much as I do, but really, thank you all for inspiring me to keep on writing. This series would be nothing without each and every one of you. I hope the Mayson clan keeps growing so that I can continue to write about them for as long as my fingers keep working.

Here's to a whole heck of a lot more BOOMS!

With all my love,

Aurora

Acknowledgments

First, I have to give thanks to God, because without him none of this would be possible. Second, I want to thank my husband. I love you now and always—thank you for believing in me even when I don't always believe in myself. To my beautiful son, you bring such joy into my life, and I'm so honored to be your mom.

To every blog and reader, thank you for taking the time to read and share my books. There would never be enough ink in the world to acknowledge you all, but I will forever be grateful to each and every one of you.

I started this writing journey after I fell in love with reading, like thousands of authors before me. I wanted to give people a place to escape where the stories were funny, sweet, and hot and left you feeling good. I have loved sharing my stories with you all, loved that I have helped people escape the real world, even for a moment.

I started writing for me and will continue writing for you. XOXO Aurora

About the Author

Aurora Rose Reynolds is a *New York Times* and *USA Today* bestselling author whose wildly popular series include Until, Until Him, Until Her, and Underground Kings.

Her writing career started in an attempt to get the outrageously alpha men who resided in her head to leave her alone and has blossomed into an opportunity to share her stories with readers all over the world.

For more information on Reynolds's latest books or to connect with her, contact her on Facebook at www.facebook.com/AuthorAuroraRoseReynolds, on Twitter @Auroraroser, or via e-mail at Auroraroser@gmail.com. To order signed books and find out the latest news, visit her at www.AuroraRoseReynolds.com or www.goodreads. com/author/show/7215619.Aurora_Rose_Reynolds.

Made in the USA
Columbia, SC
15 February 2025

53905257R00143